NO STORY TO TELL

Miles Rausch

NO STORY TO TELL

Copyright © 2020 Miles Rausch

All rights reserved.

Visit the author's website at https://www.miles.ink

For Grandma Harriet,
who created us all
out of love.

Chapter 1

It was the thought that woke Jane up. It came as a surprise to her, and she tried to blink it away the same way she blinked the dim living room into focus. But the thought remained. It hanged itself in her mind and swayed in the wind.

A lake-borne sunrise was making gray shadows haloed in pale yellow. Jane could see the photos of her grandkids on the wall, her kids, her late husband. They hung in a neat grid of fourteen, with space for more. A grandfather clock, that worked as well as she did, stood near the bookcase of westerns, the porcelain figures from dozens of Christmases and the television. She lay bundled in a recliner, a wild and twisted thing that could buck her unexpectedly. Her feet were set against the foot rest to keep her legs at a very specific angle so she could actually rest.

If today was her last, she certainly wouldn't miss sleeping in the living room. She did regret knowing there would be little time for television.

Jane freed her hands from the afghan. She examined them, holding each up so it caught the waxing light. They were small and fragile like song birds, and wrinkled and twisted like garden roots. She flexed them and teaspoons of blood began to circulate. She coughed and felt her whole body move with the air. She took a deep breath.

"Lillian?"

Jane's voice was paper-thin. It almost made no sound at all. Soon, a woman entered from the hallway. She was in her mid-forties with graying, brown hair cut short around her face. She wore silver-rimmed glasses with thin frames that sparked when they caught the light.

"Yeah, mom? Bathroom?"

Jane opened her mouth to share the thought, but nothing came out. Jane nodded instead. Lily maneuvered a walker from around the corner and set it before the chair. She gingerly pulled a lever forward to decline the foot rest. Jane lowered her feet with it, a slow, choreographed moment for both of them. With her feet on the floor, Jane gripped the end of the arm rest where the floral fabric gave way to an almond-wood finish and scooted to the edge of the seat. She took a breath.

"Doing good, mom."

Jane put her hands on the rubber grips of her walker. Lily put a hand on Jane's back. After a count of three, Jane stood. It was a slow, controlled ascent. The chair bobbed to her memory and spun a little, but Jane was free. First the right, then the left, she made the long, short journey to the bathroom.

After the bathroom, they went to the bedroom to dress. Jane found a spot on her bed and stared at her closet.

"I think I need a moment," Jane told Lily.

"Okay," said Lily. "Mind if I shower?"

Jane nodded, and Lily left that bedroom for her own. Jane's eyes perused the outfits that lined her closet. Each one was hung with memories and moments: the crisp joy of a new purchase, the shiver of silky fabric against her skin, the whisper of a compliment from John. She scanned the garments without searching. She was open to inspiration on her special occasion.

She saw it, almost right in front of her. It wasn't a dress. The weather in November constantly threatens snow, and Jane was always cold anyway. Her dresses belonged to an increasingly distant past. The chosen outfit was a blouse with matching slacks in deep purple, a rich, royal color that she'd always been feverishly drawn to. The fabric was light and strong; it was warm, and it looked like Sunday morning and felt like Sunday afternoon.

She would fetch it herself. Why shouldn't she? Dressing herself was something she'd done since the age of four. Why should ninety be any different? The walker was right next to her, and Jane was feeling sturdy today, bold even. Jane put her hands on the grips. Her arms, legs and every muscle in between tightened. She rose slowly from the bed. She pulled as much as lifted and felt herself rising to full stature.

Inch by inch she progressed up with more and more weight on those rubbery handholds.

Something shifted. It was so fast. The wheels of the walker came up, unsecured against her feeble weight, and the whole thing twisted to the right. It was slight but enough to put Jane off her balance. Jane's body did nothing but fall. She watched herself topple to the side. Jane let go and put her hands out to save herself. All she could do was wait for it all to be over.

The impact against the soft, pillowy carpet was brutal. Jane felt her wrists clack. It sent painful shocks up her arms, and she kept falling. She crumpled to her left side. The side of her head bounced. Her knees knocked together. Jane was down. The walker was up.

Jane still breathed. That was all she could do at first. The room shook like a bell. There was quite a lot of pain in her wrists. Her left elbow and shoulder hurt, too. Everything on that side was complaining. Jane's body was abandoning her, and it still rattled from the impact.

"Lillian?" Jane called. "Lillian? I need-"

Jane stopped herself. She wasn't dead yet. She felt spared. She felt awakened. She also felt time slipping away with renewed anxiety.

Jane could roll to her back. She was whole enough to do that. She'd be able to straighten out a little, take some inventory. She tried to use her right hand to push over, but the pain was too much. She tried to use her elbow but didn't have enough leverage. She reached her right arm toward the bed, groping for something she could pull. Her hand fumbled into the comforter draping from her bed. She grabbed a handful and tugged. The fabric stayed secure, and her wrist didn't ache too much. Jane took a deep breath and began to pull. Her view slowly turned. Eventually gravity helped pull her from her left side to her back. Fresh aches spidered along her left side. It was worse for the wear. Her right had come out just fine and for that she was thankful. Jane briefly considered climbing to a sitting position but decided not to press her luck.

"Lillian? Are you out there?"

"What mom?" Lily called from the living room. Jane heard the door open. "Are you done- mom!"

"What in the world! You-" Lillian was drying her hair with a beige towel as she came into the room. Lillian tossed the towel onto the bed. "Mom! Goodness! What happened?"

Lillian got behind Jane and propped her up to sitting. She threaded her arms beneath Jane's. Lily breathed a quick countdown and lifted Jane up to standing. Jane got her hands on the walker and steadied herself.

"Okay, mom?" Lily asked.

Jane nodded. "Okay."

Lily eased off the support, and Jane was standing on her own. Lily went around to the front of the walker and looked her mom up and down. She inspected each inch of the woman.

"Mom, are you okay? What happened? Are you hurt?"

Jane smiled.

"Oh, just a little tumble. I was trying some dance moves."

Lily scoffed and smiled a little.

"Dance? Yeah, right, mom. Well, no more dancing without a partner, got it?"

Jane looked around.

"You're okay, mom?"

"I think I'd like to sit again."

Lily put her hands on the walker, and Jane settled back onto the bed. Jane pointed past Lillian at the outfit in the closet.

"Which one, mom?"

"The purple."

Lillian found it and extricated it. She held it out so she could take in the color and shape of it.

"This looks nice."

"I think so, too. I want to look nice today."

"Oh, yeah? Special occasion?"

"Yes," Jane said. She cleared her throat and looked Lillian straight in the eyes. "Today, I'm going to die."

A letter from Jacob Keller to his brothers. Dated June 6, 1926.
—

To my esteemed and gracious brothers,

My family has changed again this past year. Mary Jane has given birth to our youngest, a daughter named Jane Marian. The family is doing well. Jane took sick very early on but has come out the brighter and fiercer for it. The boys have not stopped blanketing her in affections and presents. We are truly blessed.

It is along this line that I write to you all today. This letter as you read it was copied in its entirety to each of you who have a vested and financial interest in the farm. My family is now six persons and quickly outgrowing our modest dwelling. We hope to continue to grow, if God will have it for us. After some discussions with Mary Jane, I come to ask if you'll allow us to buy your shares of the family farm.

It is true that I am the youngest of us, but I am no less of a man in my thirties as are most of you. Do not picture me the runt boy of our youths, unkempt and wild. Picture me the patriarch of a small but noble family eager to take on more and give back more.

Much I have learned of farming in the past four years. I do not own land, myself, but a close friend has asked my assistance in helping with harvest and cultivation. He has described me as a quick study and solid back and can write letters to that effect. I do not presume that I can run a farm on my own, but I would eagerly devote myself to that endeavor should you all agree to it.

My final assurance is that we have the money. Under the assumption that you all accept the terms I shall outline below, we have calculated and saved to redress that very amount and procured financing for the difference. It has been a lean time in our household but such is the importance and magnitude of this opportunity.

The farm was homesteaded by our parents and ourselves. It should remain in the family, not given over to others for their safekeeping. I would move my family out there and become the caretakers of our family's legacy.

I'm proposing a twelve cents per share purchasing agreement. Without unanimous agreement, there can be no purchase. I fully present myself for the answering of any questions that arise. I shall continue my letters to moderate amongst all of you until such time as we can all meet in person.

Love and regards from your brother,
Jacob Keller

"Find it yet?" Jane yelled from the top of the stairs.

"I'm looking!" Lily yelled back.

Lily's flashlight scanned the walls looking for what her mother had described as a dark blue tote. She was in the cellar with its floor of cement and its walls of concrete and its faulty wiring.

"Mom, I'm just not-"

Jane heard Lily collide with something plastic and low to the ground.

"Found it!"

Lily carried the tote upstairs. Jane requested it be brought into her bedroom. Lily helped Jane setup on the bed then closed the door behind her to give Jane some privacy. Jane took the lid off the tote and stared down at the contents: letter after letter after letter.

Jane could only take one or two at a time. Her side was very sore, and the bending and twisting movement sent shooting pain through her body. The papers were mostly face down, and every fluttery reveal brought a new shock and memory. A poem she had written. A letter of expulsion from school. A love letter. A recipe. An obituary.

Jane started to drop the papers into piles: things written by her, things written about her, things written to her, and anything else she ran across. Her life, her story, was taking shape before her. Each new discovery twisted her up inside. What had started as a tote of memories was slowly turning into a tote of regrets and unfinished business.

"Mom? Everything going okay in there?"

"Fine," Jane said.

"I need to make some phone calls, but I wanted to check on you first."

"You can come in, Lillian."

The door opened slowly and Lily stepped inside. She took in the scene of the old lady surrounded by stacks of random papers. "What's in the box?" she asked.

Jane didn't seem to register Lily's question. "What's my story? Is it even in here?"

"Story, mom? I didn't know you wrote a story."

Jane pulled more papers out of the box, considered them, dropped them onto piles.

"I knew you wrote poems, but I didn't know you wrote a story. Is it in here? Do you want help finding it?"

Lily began to reach into the tote.

"Stop!"
Lily froze in place.
"Okay. How can I help?"
"Just give me time."
Lily screwed her face with frustration.
"Well, I'm not the one taking time away from you."
The silence was heavy.
"I'd like some privacy again."
"Mom. I'm-"
"Out, Lillian."

Lily straightened and pursed her lips. She left and the room and closed the door quietly behind her. Jane grabbed another sheet from the tote. She turned it over, and the portrait at the top startled her. The sheet fluttered from her hand and back into the tote. Large text below the man's face said, "Jackson Leo Becker."

Jane stared at the face that stared nowhere in particular. It stirred her up, and she felt fresh wounds crack open. She picked the sheet up and tossed it aside. She grabbed another and flipped it over. It was a typed letter on the impressive letterhead of Nicolas Schwartz. He was fed up with Jane and letting her know. Jane moved it aside and found another. It was a handwritten note to Santa by Rose.

The ghosts prodded her side. She felt the sins boiling inside her. Jane tossed the lid onto the tote and tried to steady her hands.

A letter from Jack Becker to Jane. Dated May 9, 1952.
—

Janey Janey:

The stories you tell are something out of this world. Once I picked them up, I couldn't stop reading. For real. There is truly so much more than your own thoughts at work. These stories were positively inspired by a higher power.

When I take the stories as part of the whole tree, they really bring a depth to the whole project. I'm not sure I want to know the answer, but I have to ask: how much of them is true? Did your great grandfather really fight off wolves with a sword in North Dakota? Did his grandfather really plow and plant every crop by hand when his two horses died unexpectedly? I don't think I want to know the truth, because they feel just too good (so, so good) to be true.

I really respect what you've created here. You're really an amazing person and writer, Janey. I can write a jazzy sentence or two, but I can't bring them to life the same way. To that end, I've left grammatical notations and included them with this letter. They are small things, and I hope you see them as my meager attempt to help perfect your beautiful stories. If all I can contribute is a comma or two, but it makes the story better, then that will be enough.

You asked how I am and how Ethel is. I've managed to spend quite a lot of time in the archives at the capitol lately and am enjoying that. Ethel has gone to be with her mother, who is not doing so well. Perhaps you've gotten some letters from her on that, so I won't share all the details here. To keep myself occupied, I dig into this research. I'm getting such a taste for it that I shouldn't be surprised if I take up this project for my own family after we've completed this work. I feel that every family should maintain an exhaustive history, and I applaud you for taking on yours.

Have you given any consideration to working on this in person with me? I am perfectly willing to travel, and it would be much easier to collaborate in person. I do very much enjoy your company. I shouldn't presume that you enjoy mine, but we could work in as much silence as you wish. My supplies and tools are easily transported, and we can discuss some important visual details about the project. Please consider it.

I heartily welcome any new stories you've conceived, and I shall return them with the considerably minor corrections they warrant.

Give my brother and nephews my love.

Yours truly,
Jumping Jack Flash

Lily was on the cream-colored wall phone in the kitchen. She cupped the receiver and spoke in hushed, panicked whispers, pacing a small semicircle of kitchen. The cord danced the distance.

"I swear that's what I heard," Lily said. "Then she asked me to bring up a box of old letters and stuff… What could she mean? … No, I'm sure that's what she said. … Well, which one of us was actually here, JJ?"

Jane was in her chair again. A western played on the TV and toast sat partially eaten in front of her. She had the volume down to better overhear Lily in the other room.

"No, not suicidal. Normal. Like she was saying, "I'm going to the cafe today."… Her sodium is fine, JJ. I already talked to Rose about- … Because she's a doctor, and you're a real estate agent. … Well, I'm freaked out, too!"

Jane turned the volume up. She didn't need to hear the anxiety she was producing in her children. This wasn't about getting attention. This just was.

"I think we need to keep an extra eye on her. … No, I don't think she'll do anything, but… Maybe she can feel that something is off, you know. People know their bodies. … Maybe it's not something we can fix but it's something we can react to, you know? … Okay. I'll keep you posted. You might need to be on call. If she needs me, I can get a sub, but I'd rather not, you know. … Yeah, okay. I'll let you know. … Thanks, JJ."

Lily hung up and came into the living room.

"Mom, are you-"

"When do you have to head to school?" Jane asked.

Lily twisted her mouth into a disapproving pucker. She looked at her watch.

"I can get a sub."

"I don't need a babysitter. I'm not suicidal, just practical. When do you have to leave?"

"I should leave in fifteen minutes."

"Would you take me to church first?"

"You'll be pretty early."

Jane smiled. "A couple extra Hail Mary's won't kill me."

Lily raised her eyebrows but didn't laugh.

"That was a joke, Lillian. My sense of humor still works."

Lily looked off into the distance for a moment. Then she nodded.

"Let me get my bag."

Lily disappeared upstairs. She returned a couple moments later with her bag and coat. She fetched Jane's from the front entry and brought it to the chair. Then she wheeled the walker over, and they began their dance. Jane was leaning forward, arms braced on the walker, pushing up to stand when a sudden, sharp pain struck her left side. She froze. The strike was fast and cruel and took a precious dram of energy. But she didn't gasp.

"Okay, mom?" Lily asked.

Jane gave a curt nod and pushed through the pain to standing. She gave her youngest a shaky smile.

"Is it your fall, mom? Did you get hurt?"

Jane shook Lily's question off.

"Can I check? See if you're okay?"

"No," Jane said, making the word into granite. Lily eyed her mother, but Jane ignored it and started toward the kitchen.

"Let's get going," Jane said. "I don't want you to be late."

"Mom, I can take the day-"

"Race you," Jane called out. Lily fetched the coat from the chair and followed her mom out the back, draping it across the old woman's shoulders before she stepped out into the winter.

Chapter 2

From an early age, Jane found a transcendent comfort in the straightforward, functional facade of St. Thomas Aquinas Catholic Church. The building had changed remarkably little in the hundred years it had housed parishioners. Brown double doors below a peaked bell tower. A roof in the shape of an inverted-v. Its lines were straight and right. Its surfaces were cut into simple shapes that admitted quick construction. Only paints and fabrics had faded. What had once been white was now a light ash, once mauve pew cushions were now puce.

Lily drove her SUV up a small driveway that lead to the handicap ramp. In six minutes flat, they were out of the car and shuffling up the ramp. Lily went around the lamp to the front steps and, when Jane was close enough, Lily opened one of the double doors and secured it open by means of a small hooked chain attached to the railing.

There was a lip of wood and metal to clear before getting inside. Lily and Jane negotiated it carefully. It was another small reminder to Jane that her body was no longer her own. She felt a small needle of pity prod her side. She shook it off and continued into the building. She waved a dismissive hand behind her.

"You head to school, Lillian. I'll be fine."

"But… mom, are you sure? I can walk you-"

"I'm sure," Jane said. "I'm in good hands."

"Okay, mom. JJ is going to pick you up and bring you wherever you need to go after mass, okay?"

Jane nodded but Lily didn't see it. Jane was too taxed from her efforts to speak or turn around. She just needed to sit a while and let her side settle down.

"I'll see you after school, mom."

The door closed, and Jane stopped. It was dark. She waited for her eyes to adjust. Mass was nearly an hour away, and very few of the lights were on. The heat certainly wasn't, and Jane was glad for the coat around her shoulders. She was in the anteroom. Ahead of her waited another set of double doors. One door had been propped open. She was thankful for that. She padded into the church to find her pew.

The church was bigger on the inside. Overlooking the congregation was the choir loft. Jane had spent decades up there, before she started her family and after they'd flown away. She shuffled in its shadow now. She loved it up there, perched in the balcony. Up high is where songbirds sit, and Jane was one of the sweetest. She boasted a dulcet soprano and gave her talents to every Sunday mass she could. The faithful were shrinking every year, and the choir even faster. Jane felt it was her duty to sing. She didn't have much else to give.

The pews for the congregation were arranged in two wide columns with an aisle dividing them. You could fit two or three families per row, or one row of Beckers, Jane used to say. They would sit near the front when the kids were young, so that the sunlight cascading through the stained glass windows would splash onto her family. On dark winter mornings, the saints were barely visible.

Jane didn't have a pew any longer. She had a chair, borrowed from the church hall, that was set behind the rows of pews. Father had even had her name put on it using the same label maker that named everything in the sacristy: EUCHARISTS, HYMNALS, JANE BECKER. The chair had been carefully left in the exact proper spot for her to transition from the walker on her own. She pushed over to it and rotated her body into position, tiny step by tiny step. She reached tentative hands behind her onto the chair's arms. She counted to herself: 1, 2, 3. Then she slumped onto the padded seat.

Jane relaxed. The needle was withdrawing. Her side was getting more tender and frustrated. She gingerly felt along her left side; it was all bruised. Jane's hand went to her coat pocket. She found a small leather bag with a zipper. She unzipped it and shook out the chain of beads that were inside. Her fingers unwound the purple mess, and she stretched it to its rightful shape. It was her favorite rosary, a wedding gift from John. She draped the decades over her hand and found the crucifix. Jane closed her eyes and began to pray.

A letter from Mary Jane Keller to her mother. Dated August 11, 1932.
—

Dearest mother,

My sweet darling Jane has been a shell of herself lately. Since the fire, she's been a shade wandering amongst us. She has very little interest in activities of any kind, especially physical. She shows little interest in talking and even less in eating. It is a fight to get her to come down to supper every night. Perhaps worst, she has stopped writing and stopped taking an interest in anything literary or imaginative.

Jacob supposes that she perhaps breathed in too much smoke that night, but I see no way that could be the cause. In any case, wouldn't we all be lethargic and helpless like this? We all stood in a line watching the orange blaze in the night. We all breathed the same char and embers.

Jacob has been a madman about rebuilding the barn, and the boys always mimic his fervor. Janey, however, is always a different story. She loves her father. She worships him. But she does not always follow him to his ends. Yet, this fire seems to have taken all that passion out of her. She has no form. She is like clay left forgotten on the wheel. Ironic that a fire should turn such a fierce, strong thing back into clay. Fire turns real clay into pottery.

Can I ever expect her to return to us? I know it's impossible for you to tell, but your words are always so comforting to me. Seven days have passed, and she shows no indication of getting better. Should I call on the doctor to inspect her? Should I ask Father Fischer to pray over her? Perhaps there is a medicine or prayer we can employ to rouse the old Jane from the clutches of this one.

The truth of the matter is, the fire was her fault. She was writing in the barn with a lantern. When I called for supper, she must have knocked the lamp over. I doubt she even knew it. The kerosene and flame took hold almost immediately. Before we knew it, the barn was aflame in our very own backyard. Such a sight I'd never seen. I would think it beautiful were it not so detrimental to our family.

Jane must feel some guilt, maybe much, but even in her most flagrant of previous transgressions her response to guilt was nothing like this. If anything, confronted with the truth of her actions, Jane's typical response has been to react in anger and expressions of defiance. Confrontation makes her balloon up, not shrink away. That is why this is so baffling.

Even her brothers have noticed a change. James asked me if she'd come down with another disease. She was so sickly as a child, as you know. Joshua wondered if she'd been stung or bit by something recently. Joseph wondered if he could shake the melancholy out of her. I declined his offer.

I eagerly await your thoughts and guidance on this matter. We are all eager to get our Janey back.

With all of my love,
Mary Jane

Jane was saying a Hail Mary when Father touched her shoulder.

"I'm so sorry to interrupt you, Jane. I just wanted to say good morning."

Jane put her hand on top of father's and did her best to squeeze it.

"Good morning, father," Jane croaked. Her voice was sandpaper from disuse. Father patted her shoulder and started down the center aisle. Father Garcia was a short man, and round. He waddled a little when he walked, and his face was always flushed with the effort of mobility. In her younger days, she may have disdained him for that. Now she knew too well how the body can betray. Father was kind and thoughtful and barely looked his sixty years of age.

"Father?"

Father Garcia stopped and waddled back to her. "Yes, Jane?"

"Are you hearing confessions today?"

"I certainly can. Would you like to meet before mass or after?"

"Before, Father. If you have the time."

"I have plenty of time. How much do you have left?"

Jane froze, thinking he was asking how much time she had left. He nodded at Jane's rosary, and she understood. She lifted the beads and counted.

"Two decades."

"I'll be ready before you're done, then."

Jane smiled at Father and head down the aisle, genuflect and cross to the sacristy door. She intended to return to her rosary but found she couldn't focus. She wished she had paper and a pen to jot down the forgotten sins needling her side. Small sins danced in and out of her memory. Long forgotten ones rekindled themselves. The guilt seized her heart and skipped a beat.

"Jane?"

Jane started. Father was back, extending a hand for her. Jane took a deep breath, and they got her up and into the walker. Her side stung with the motion, but it wasn't as bad as before. Maybe she was healing already. They walked to the confessional, a small room built into the back of the church. Inside was a screen and kneeler for guarded confessions or two chairs for bolder ones. Jane chose the chair. Father closed the door behind them. He rolled her walker out of the way and took his seat, facing her. He set his Bible, dog-eared and bulging with ribbons, on a table near them. Jane noticed it was not unlike her own.

Father centered himself. He began the sign of the cross. Jane followed.

"Let's begin in the name of the Father, and of the Son, and of the Holy Spirit."

"Amen," Jane answered. "Bless me, Father, for I have sinned. It has been three weeks since my last confession, and eighty-four years since my sin."

Jane closed her eyes and began to share.

A letter from John Becker, Sr. to Jane. Dated September 23, 1950.
—

Blue J:

The further north they march us, the more frightened I become. I know what's up there waiting for us: the enemy. It's not just me feeling fate closing in on us. Almost everyone in the company is having nightmares or trouble sleeping. I sleep just fine (I always have), but I have this vivid vision of horrible things happening to the men around me.

We might be marching up a road in two single file lines, weapons at ready. We're all in our uniforms. We're all sunburned. The sweat collects under the collar. I can feel the sweat snake down my spine. A guy might catch my eye because of the way he's running or holding his weapon, and I'll suddenly see his head blown off. Or I'll see him spontaneously explode in front of me. Or I'll picture a bayonet coming up through his sternum. Any number of horrible things play before my eyes, just as clearly as if they really happened. I blink until they disappear, but they keep happening.

I want to talk to the medic about it, but I'm worried they'll flag me with something. I want to talk to the priest about it, but I'm worried he'll say I'm possessed or something. That means you're the first person I've told. Hopefully the last. Hopefully the dreams go away soon. We should be getting some downtime in the next week. Maybe that'll help.

To pass the time as I march, I've been writing to you in my head. I've been writing poetry. I know! I'm surprised by it, too. I guess you're not the only poet in our little family. I've never thought much about poetry until this war. Now I'm lousy with it. Here's my latest poem. I hope it makes you smile.

Dearest Janey, cast so far
    Your face is prettiest by far
    I will buy you a golden bar
    If I ever survive this stupid war.

Dearest Janey, my darling wife
    You have made a perfect wife
    I will save you from all strife
    If I ever survive with my life.

* * *

Dearest Janey, smart and great
    Your burden at home must be so great
    I hope I don't get home late
    If I ever survive this fate.

Dearest Janey, from the barn
    You are like a farmer's barn
    Keeper and teller of the yarns
    I hope I escape from harm.

Dearest Janey, cast so far
    Your face is prettiest by far
    I will buy you a golden bar
    If I ever survive this stupid war.

Dearest, deepest love,
    John

When mass concluded, Jane waited for everyone to leave. She smiled and shook hands and endured doleful glances from the friends and acquaintances who filed past her. Some of them seemed to know what she did, and she wondered if she was wearing it on her face, in the weighted slump of her posture. When everyone had passed by her, the church was empty. Jane began the mutter the remainder of her rosary.

She felt a hand on her shoulder.

"Hey, mom," said John, Jr. He swooped around to kiss her on the cheek. "Ready to go?"

Jane smiled at him. John, as a young man, had been thin and lanky. Now that he neared seventy, there was a sagging thinness to his body. He was balding on top but retained a wreath of close cut brown and silver hair and a neat beard. His facial features were pointed in a way that made him look slightly professorial, although he'd never taught a day in his life. She tucked the beads back into their bag.

"I have one more thing I'd like to do."

"Oh?"

"I'd like to sing."

John shrugged. "Okay. Go ahead. A-one, two, three, Happy birthday…"

Jane narrowed her eyes and cocked her head at him, a gesture she had cultivated in years of suffering his chicanery. He gave her a rueful smile, the closest he ever got to admitting he was aggravating his mother.

"Okay, what do you mean?"

"I need your help getting up."

Jane pointed to the balcony above them.

"You want to go up the stairs?"

"Yes."

"Into the choir loft?"

"Yes."

"Is this related to your… morning revelation?"

Jane said, matter-of-factly, "I'm going to die today, John, and I'd like to sing upstairs one last time."

John sighed. He held his hand out for her.

"Whatever you say, lady."

He helped her up and into her walker, and they walked to the choir loft steps. John opened the door and surveyed the steep climb.

"I have an idea that you won't like, so I'm not going to share it with you."

"What?"

John walked around the walker. He put one arm against Jane's back, and the other arm he swept into her knees. Jane cried out in surprise as John tucked her into his arms.

"Going up," he said as he made his way sideways up the narrow stairwell. Jane put her arm on his shoulder and considered how much like John, Sr., her son was.

She realized that she might see John tomorrow, and it took her breath away.

"Here we are," John, Jr., said, setting Jane down gingerly in front of a music stand. It was the music stand she always sang from, denuded of music.

"Need a beat?" John asked? He started to beatbox behind a hand cupped over his mouth.

Jane put a hand on his shoulder.

"Find the Ave Maria."

John grabbed a hymnal from one of the choir loft pews and flipped through it.

"Any idea what number?"

"670."

"Wow. Okay…"

John flipped to 670 and set the hymnal on the music stand in front of his mother. She smoothed the binding with a shaky hand. She took a deep breath. She closed her eyes and opened her mouth to sing the first haunting, soaring note of the hymn.

Nothing happened.

Jane cleared her throat and tried again. Air came out, but none of her music. Jane felt her eyes sting.

"Okay, mom?"

Jane cleared her throat again, but a truth occurred to her, and she closed the book.

"Yes, Junior. I'm okay. I'm ready to go."

John frowned. "Are you sure?"

"I'm sure. We can go."

"I thought you wanted to sing."

"I did," Jane said, "I wanted to sing one last song. I just didn't realize I'd already done it."

Chapter 3

Jane picked up her mug and blew a shallow breath across the top. She took a sip. Jane felt the hot liquid coating her throat, her stomach, her entire body. She started to feel warm for once.

Jane listened to the conversation around her. Her friends took their turns offering and bolstering and disparaging their topics. She was content to let the familiar music of their voices sing to her. As they talked, she reached for some sugar packets in the center of the table. She used one in her coffee and pocketed the rest. She listened.

Marilyn, to Jane's right, was squat and round with a kindly face but terse disposition. She stared at the phone in her hand while adding in what she wanted to the conversation. To Jane's left was Ethel. Ethel was tall and beautiful and creased with smile and worry lines. Her hands spent most of their time covering her mouth. Next to Ethel was Judith. Judith, a small, frail-looking thing with bold makeup, a fierce beak and an unrelenting gaze, was holding court.

"I've had it," she said. "I'm done with bridge. I mean it. I really am."

Judith's hand sliced the air in violent condemnation. Ethel recoiled from the gesture and frowned in phantom pain. Marilyn nodded.

"What's wrong with bridge? It's a lovely," offered Ethel. "I find it very relaxing. Especially when the arthritis acts up, and I can't knit a thing."

"I agree," grunted Marilyn. "Don't play bridge if you can help it."

"Marilyn, is there a card game you do enjoy?"

Marilyn frowned in thought. She shook her head.

"Is there any game you enjoy?"

"There must have been one, but they probably don't make it anymore."

Ethel turned back to Judith and cocked her head in genuine concern. "What did bridge do wrong, Judith?"

"The game is rigged. Must be. My team never wins."

"Where do you play?"

"At the home."

Marilyn snorted. "'Course it's rigged."

Judith swung a hand in Marilyn's direction. "See? Marilyn knows."

"Skimp on the food, too. Especially for guests."

"See? Marilyn's on my side."

"And I'm not entirely sure they've been given you the right pills."

"Okay, Marilyn. You can be a little less on my side now."

Ethel waved them off.

"Who do you play with?"

"Doesn't seem to matter. No matter what partner I get, we always lose."

"Same ladies every time?"

"Not just ladies, but yes. Same crew every time."

"And your team always loses?"

"Every darn time, Ethel. It's a darn conspiracy."

"Well..." Ethel dipped a toe into cold, uncertain waters. "It could be something else."

"Bad cards? Crooked deck?"

"Not exactly..."

Ethel couldn't bring herself to say it.

"She says it's you," grunted Marilyn. "You suck at cards."

Judith's eyes grew twice their size. She recoiled from the statement and crossed her arms across her floral print blouse and purple jacket. Her hat, a jaunty, Kentucky Derby-type thing, threatened to unseat itself. Her mud brown eyes were darkened to spots of coal with anger.

"I never-"

"She's got a point," Marilyn muttered. "You're awful at solitaire, too."

Judith's eyes grew to half her face. Her mouth gaped. When she realized, she snapped it shut. Judith grabbed her mug and took an angry sip, glaring at Ethel and Marilyn.

"Bridge is a fine game, but it all depends on your partner," Ethel said. She nodded in finality. "Have you tried pinochle? It's not nearly as heavy as bridge, and it's mostly luck. So, if you lack-"

"What do I possibly lack, Ethel? You forget how fabulous I am."

Judith's face was as serious as the grave.

"Of course, dear," said Ethel, patting Judith on the hand. She took a sip of her coffee.

"Marilyn," said Judith, "what do you play to pass the time?"

"Poker," Marilyn grunted.

"Oh, dear," said Ethel.

"Only true card game there is."

"Do you ever make money?" asked Judith.

Marilyn smiled from one side of her mouth. "I usually have a little skin in the game."

Judith leaned forward with interest. "It's been ages since I played… What kind of poker do you play? Five card draw?"

Marilyn's small, dark eyes twinkled at Judith. "Not quite. But it's a popular kind."

"Seven card stud? Texas hold 'em?"

Marilyn's smile broke across her entire face.

"Strip," she pronounced. She winked.

Judith guffawed. Ethel gasped. Her hand went to her chest, clutching some imaginary pearls.

"Oh, it's not so bad, Ethel," Marilyn added. "But you might want to leave before the after-party. That's when the fun really begins."

Judith cackled and slapped her knee. Ethel's jaw dropped and her pale cheeks bloomed.

"You have five kids, Ethel. It hasn't been that long, has it?"

Ethel could only shake her head in silence

"Jane, save me from this filth," Ethel begged. She reached a hand out and placed it on Jane's arm. "What have you been up to? What's new?"

"Well," Jane began, setting her mug onto the table, "I'm about to leave, and I wanted to see everyone before I left."

"Oh, that's lovely," Ethel said. "We love having you."

"Where are you going?" asked Judith.

"To see John, I hope!" Jane chirped. She laughed alone.

"Janey…" said Ethel.

"Is it cancer?" asked Judith.

"Cancer's a bitch," growled Marilyn. "Took Henry in six months. Cancer's a bitch."

"Is it cancer, Janey?" Ethel squeezed Jane's arm.

Jane shook her head. She stared at her coffee a moment, swimming in the oily swirl.

"You know when you're playing Solitaire, and you're only a couple moves in but you already know you're going to win?"

The ladies nodded.

"I woke up with that feeling today."

"Clearing the cards," said Marilyn.

"No," barked Judith, frowning. "You're not clearing the cards. You're throwing the game."

"Judith!" Ethel scolded. "Let the woman pass in peace."

"I'll do no such thing. You don't get to die, Jane. You're just too… You matter too much to us."

They nodded again in solemn unison. Jane smiled at them. She could only meet their gaze for a moment before diving back into the coffee.

"I'll ask John to just wait a little longer then?" Jane asked. "Would that be fair?"

Jane didn't look up to see, but Judith blinked fiercely and found an interesting scene across the cafe. Some color came into her face.

"What's next on your schedule?"

"I'd love to take a nap, but I don't think I dare," Jane chuckled. Light smiles brightened the table. Ethel squeezed Jane's arm again. Marilyn reached over and squeezed the other one. Judith stretched across the table and took Jane by the hands. They held each other for a moment like that, surrounded by their coffee in the middle of the weekday crowd.

"Should I round you up a poker game?" Marilyn asked, and she winked.

A letter from Shammi Kumar to Jane. Dated July 5, 1965.
—

Dear Jane,

I shall have no opposition from you. I am giving you the Mangalore book. I saw you pouring over it when you visited last Sunday, and we had such a wonderful talk afterwards that I insist that you have it.

This is not unusual for me. I let books fly into my life and fly out again. And when I meet a new friend who feels in my soul like an old friend, I must give them a part of me that they may remember us as we were in that moment.

You remember? We were sitting in my kitchen, and the sunlight was blinding me. I asked you if we could change chairs, and you were gracious enough to allow that. When we sat back down, I saw the sunlight pour through your hair, and your face had such light in it. I knew that you were a special creature, Jane Becker.

We talked only a little about curry, because we were in such a hurry to discuss so much else in our lives. In this book is a recipe for a dish called "ball curry." It is such a horrible name for something so fantastic. It is a meat kofta curry, which means that it is a meatball curry. The recipe combines so many of the most important flavors of India: it is sweet, savory and spicy all in one dish. It is an experience, and it brings me to my home and my mother's kitchen every time. It is not difficult to make, but it takes care and respect.

When I reflected on our conversation, I saw something else in that face: you are weary, Jane. I hear fight in your voice, but I see resignation in your smile. I implore you, do not let them knock you down. I do not know who they are, but I see their marks upon your face. I grew up seeing this in the women around me.

My mother, grandmother, aunts all wore those same creased masks. Those masks take you over, Jane Becker. When I left, my mother's mask and face were inseparable. Masks are horrid things. They obstruct your vision. They color your scents with your own breath. They eliminate your ability to feel emotion. I came here to escape masks.

When I met you, I realized that women cannot escape masks but we can stop them. We can push the mask away. Push, Jane Becker! Never stop pushing!

I apologize for such a short letter but life threatens to wash me away again. I hope for many blessings upon you and your house, and best luck in making the curry.

Sincerely and ever your friend,
Shammi Kumar

James left when John, Jr., returned. James wanted to get back to work. He kissed Jane gently on the cheek and made one last stooping search for the cardinal. It was gone. Junior brought in bags of groceries. He carried them to the kitchen counter and began to empty them. Junior stopped James before he left, spoke to him earnestly, and James nodded.

"What's this?" asked Jane.

"I thought we could have supper here. We'll invite the whole family. Well, everyone who's around. I'll cook. You can relax."

"Don't you have work?"

"Houses aren't going anywhere. It's not like Becker Real Estate is going to collapse, because I took the day off. It stayed the course just fine when dad passed away, and it'll do the same when you do."

"What about James? Why does he have to go back."

"Well, he doesn't. But he feels better when he's on a schedule, so I told him when supper is, and he'll be fine."

Jane thought about protesting. She felt like too much of a bother all of a sudden. But she didn't have the energy to fight it.

"What are you making me?"

"Figured I'd slow cook some ribs, grill some burgers and brats."

"In November?"

"You deserve one last cookout."

Junior smiled at her, but there was something in his eyes when he smiled.

"Still feel pretty certain this is your last day on earth?"

Jane looked out the window. She reached inside and out and tried to find an answer to that question. That thought remained. She nodded. Junior shrugged.

"Alright. Grill out it is."

"What about sides?"

"James is going to mix up some baked beans. Beck is going to make some coleslaw and green bean casserole. Hillary will bring fruit salad."

Junior cleared the bags of their contents. He folded the brown paper sacks neatly back along their lines and walked them into the mudroom out back. When he returned, he started to put some of the items into the fridge, some he started to unwrap, the rest he set aside.

"You and Lily can just relax."

"No, I can't relax."

"That's about the only thing you can do. And it's the only thing you should be doing. Maybe that feeling that you're going to die today is stress. Or anxiety. Hillary gets panic attacks. Could be something like that."

Jane wanted to be unambiguous in her movements. She set her jaw and shook her head.

"I can't explain where the thought came from, Junior, but it wasn't from me. It wasn't a voice of fear or panic. It was a voice of calm."

"It could be something else."

"Like what?"

"You're getting older-"

"You keep saying that."

"Well, it could be the fear of what's next."

"I've heard the voice of fear of death, John," Jane said cooly. "It kept me up for weeks while your dad wasted away."

A slab of ribs lay on a cloth before Junior. He stopped rubbing the orange and red and black spices into the marbled flesh. His hands were stained. He stared into space.

Junior chewed his lower lip for a moment. "I know that voice, too," he said. He turned to face his mother. "Okay. I believe you."

Jane sighed in relief. A thin smile brightened her face.

"Thank you, John."

Junior went back to the meat. He finished the rub and wrapped it in plastic. He pulled out a baking sheet and settled the ribs onto it. Then the whole thing went into the fridge. Junior swung the fridge door shut in triumph.

"I'll let that marinade for an hour, then I'll throw them on the grill."

"Good," Jane said. "Help me up. Get the walker."

Junior grabbed the walker and set it before her. He helped her rise up. She pushed herself over and into the kitchen.

"Mom, what are you doing?"

"Does Dane still love my bread pudding?"

"He asks me to get some every time I mention coming over here."

"Okay, then. Open the bread box."

Jane turned the oven to 350 degrees. Junior discovered portions from three different loaves of bread.

"What's left?"

"Half a loaf of whole wheat. Part of a sourdough. Three slices of white."

Jane frowned.

"I was hoping for some brioche."

"Well, then you should've bought some brioche. Want me to go out?"

Jane thought about the breads, their various flavors and textures and properties.

"No, I can make this work. Hand them over."

"Okey-dokey," Junior said, pulling the bags out of the bread box. "What now?"

"Eggs, milk, butter, vanilla, sugar and salt."

As Jane rattled off the ingredients, Junior threw open cabinet and fridge doors to locate them. Almost as quickly as she could say them, he had them lined up on the counter.

"What's next?"

"Saucepan, baking dish, whisk, measuring cups, measuring spoons."

"Done and done."

The utensils were lined as neatly as the ingredients. Jane could get to them with ease.

"Okay, now go away."

Junior snorted. "What? Go away?"

"My recipe is a long-held secret, Junior. I'm not about to give it away now. Scooch."

Junior's mouth gaped open. He looked around for someone to validate the ludicrous situation. Jane just stared at him humorlessly. At last, Junior dropped his head and slumped out of the room. When she heard the TV in the living room change stations, she knew she could proceed. Jane opened a cupboard near the fridge and grabbed a bottle of brandy and set it with the rest of the ingredients.

Jane whisked and mixed and baked like she was ten years younger. Young enough to stand a little way from the walker, to stand a little straighter, to stir with a tad more vigor. In no time, she had the bread pudding mixed and ready. She slid the baking dish carefully across the metal rack into the oven. She admired it for a moment, this delicious piecemeal dessert. Then she closed the oven door and set the timer for forty-five minutes. She returned the brandy to its hiding spot.

Jane's eye caught a small box tucked into the corner where two countertop pieces met. She snagged the box and opened it. It was a small, wooden recipe box, baby blue and ancient. She thumbed through the recipes and pulled out a lightly worn but equally ancient index card. It was written in the hand of her youth: confident, agile, careless. Across the top was written, "Jane's Bread Pudding." She put the recipe into her pocket and gave it a soft pat.

"Junior," Jane called out, "we have an errand to run."

A recipe for bread pudding by Rebecca Nowack. Undated.

—

Rebecca's Bread Pudding

Ingredients:
- 2 cups of milk
- 2 tablespoons of butter
- 1 teaspoon of vanilla
- 1 teaspoon of cinnamon
- 1 teaspoon of allspice
- 1/2 cup of sugar
- 2 eggs
- 1/2 loaf of leftover bread, torn into ragged pieces
- A dash of salt
- A dusting of cinnamon
- A dusting of sugar

Preparation:
1) Heat the oven to 350 degrees.
2) In a saucepan with low heat, mix the milk, butter, vanilla, cinnamon, allspice, sugar and salt. When the butter has melted and the sugar has dissolved, set aside.
3) Grease a four-cup baking dish.
4) Fill the dish with bread chunks.
5) When milk mixture is cooled, whisk the eggs into it.
6) Pour the whole over the bread evenly.
7) Bake for forty-five minutes. The custard should still wobble. Bread will be browned.
8) Dust with powdered sugar and cinnamon.
9) Serve warm.

A recipe for bread pudding by Jane Becker. Undated.
—

Jane's Bread Pudding

Ingredients:
- 2 cups of milk
- 2 tablespoons of butter
- 1 teaspoon of vanilla
- 1/3 cup of sugar
- 2 eggs
- 1/2 loaf of sweet bread (brioche, pref.) cut into 2-inch cubes
- A pinch of salt
- A dusting of sugar
- A dusting of cinnamon
- 1/4 cup of brandy

Preparation:
1) Heat the oven to 350 degrees.
2) Over low heat, whisk milk, butter, vanilla, brandy, sugar and salt. When the butter has melted and the sugar has dissolved, set aside to cool.
3) Grease a four-cup baking dish and fill it with bread cubes. Use larger pieces along the outside for a nice crust.
4) When milk is cooled, beat the eggs and whisk them into the liquid.
6) Pour the liquid over the bread.
7) Bake for forty-five minutes. The custard should still wobble a little and the bread will be browned.
8) Dust with powdered sugar and cinnamon.
9) Serve warm.

When they got back home, the timer for the bread pudding had three minutes remaining. Jane walked herself into the kitchen and over to the oven. She tried to bend over to see the progress through the frosted black window, but a sharp pain cut into her side. She lost her breath for a moment and stood quickly just as Junior came into the room.

"Did we burn it?"

Jane tried to hide her gulps for air.

"Nope. Two minutes left."

"Wow! That's lucky!" Junior said.

Her lungs returned to work. She relaxed.

"Lucky?" Jane said. "Why do you think it was luck, young man?"

Junior rolled his eyes at his mom's beaming smile.

"Can you take it out for me, dear?"

Junior pulled the bread pudding out and set it on the stove top. Jane used an oven mitt to hold one corner of the pan. She gave it a suddenly jerk, and the bread pudding shimmied. She tapped a finger against the crust. It was hard and made a hollow "thuck" sound. She touched a finger lightly to the custard and found it giving and moist.

"Perfect," Jane said. "Hand me a towel, please."

Junior fetched a white dish towel from one of the drawers. Jane tossed it over the bread pudding and set it back on the stove to make room.

"All yours," Jane said. She turned and walked herself into the other room. She could hear the opening and closing of the fridge, the crinkle of plastic wrap, the clang of pots and pans. Junior was giving the ribs one last rub before taking them out to the grill. Jane positioned herself in front of her chair, facing away from it. She reached one hand behind her, aiming for the arm. The screen door in the mud room slammed. Jane's hand touched fabric. She tried to grab it, but it bobbed out of reach. The chair rotated and hit her legs which were very sensitive. The pain gave her knees out, and Jane was falling. She hit the chair and clutched the arms for dear life. The wind went out of her. She held on, praying the chair wouldn't eject her. It swiveled and shook and stopped when it banged against the phone table.

Jane had to gasp a couple of times to get her breath back this second time. The room was spinning, and her side hurt more than before. She had mostly forgotten about the injury, and her side craved the attention. When the chair was steady, Jane reached an arm under her shirt. She was surprised by the wetness. When she pulled her hand out, it was dark with blood. Some of it was clotted, but some of it was new. She grabbed a tissue from the side table and cleaned her hand.

The screen door opened again. Jane heard Junior working in the kitchen for a moment before going back out. Jane steeled herself and reached for the handholds on her walker. With great effort, she stood. She walked herself into the bathroom and closed the door.

Jane washed her hands. The blood washed away, pass by pass. She dried her hands. She went for the first aid kit tucked into a drawer of the vanity. She got out gauze and tape. Jane pulled her shirt up as high as she could and looked over the damage. She was dark maroon, and the shape her body wasn't right.

Jane reached for toilet paper but caught sight of some ugly but matching hand towels. Jane grabbed one and mopped up the blood. It looked much better cleaned. She couldn't tell where she was bleeding or if she still was. She'd do her best anyway. Jane rifled through the kit for gauze. She held it against her skin and applied the tape. She added perpendicular strips of tape to keep it secure. When she was done, she made herself decent, tossed her wrappers, and replaced the first aid kit.

Jane was falling apart.

Chapter 4

Jane and Junior climbed into his vehicle, following their careful choreography. Junior started to head out of Stone City toward Meridian proper.

"Can I take some guesses?"

"Sure."

"Candy. Just boxes and boxes of it."

"Why would I go to the bank to withdraw candy?"

"Because they always have some there. And because you never let us have any when we were kids. We had to beg for it. And I imagine that any candy you intercepted went to the bank for posterity."

Jane chuckled.

"No? Okay, a puppy then."

"Oh, Junior."

"We begged and begged you for a dog and you wouldn't get us one. You must have gotten one. How could you resist all those adorable faces? But you were just waiting for us to earn it, and we were too hellish to deserve it, so you kept it in a safe deposit box."

"You can't keep living things in those boxes."

"And how would you know that unless you tried. And… and failed! You killed our puppy! How could you?? And this is how you tell me??"

Jane smile was amused but tired.

"Okay, I have one more. Is it dad?"

Jane's smile faded and nothing replaced it.

"Oh, come on, mom. I'm just joking. You already said they can't keep living things in safe deposit boxes."

Junior felt his skin crawling in the silence. He stared straight ahead. Jane was a thousand miles away. She blinked and returned.

"I'm going to tell him all about these funny jokes of yours. He'll have a word or two for you when you come home."

"Eeesh. What's he going to do? Haunt me?"

Jane just smirked.

The car crept downtown. Giant buildings seemed to grow up out of the soil like huge, metal crops. The streets were lined with cars despite it being the middle of the afternoon on a work day. Junior pulled into the parking garage for the bank. They made their way slowly from the vehicle into the bank storefront.

Jennifer Spalding was Jane's preferred teller, and she was busy at the moment. Rather than move to any of the open tellers, Junior and Jane waited in Jennifer's line. When it was their turn, Jennifer greeted them both by name beaming a huge smile.

"I'd like to see my safe deposit box, please, Jennifer" Jane said.

"Okay. I'll just need to see your ID, and I can fetch it for you. Do you have the key?"

Jane looked at Junior who fished the keychain out of his pocket. He handed it to Jane who located the correct one and held it up. Jennifer nodded and disappeared for a moment and returned with a form. She set it on the shelf in front of Jane and indicated with an X where Jane should sign authorizing the retrieval of the box.

Jennifer jerked her head toward Junior. "Are you letting this one in with you?"

Jane smirked and pretended to consider it.

"Mom, think of the puppy," Junior said, folding his hands together in prayer.

"Puppy?" Jennifer asked.

"Yes, he can come in," Jane said.

Jennifer pointed at another line further down. "Print his name here, and sign here."

When the paper was signed, Jennifer whisked it away into the back again. When she returned, she beckoned them to follow her. She came around the railing and escorted them out of the teller area to a hallway of rooms. The hallway was dim. The walls were punctuated by numbered doors on both sides. Little signs hung them that read either "OCCUPIED" or "VACANT." Jennifer lead them to vacant room 109.

She held the door open for them. Then Jennifer closed the door behind them.

In the middle of the room was a wooden table. Junior helped Jane onto one of the cold and poorly padded folding chairs. Junior stood along one of the plain, dark gray walls. Junior took out his cellphone to pass the time, but there was no signal and no wifi. There was a knock, a pause and the door opened. Jennifer was back with two guards. Jennifer held the door open as the guards carried the box between them. They rested it on the table before Jane, then they left.

"I'll leave here in a minute so you two can be alone with your possessions," Jennifer said. "Before I do, is there anything I can do for either of you?"

"Guinness?"

Jennifer laughed but didn't answer. Jane shook her head, and Jennifer left them alone.

Junior stood at the table. Jane pulled the key from her pocket. She opened the box and threw the lid open so Junior could see everything inside.

"What the hell is that?"

Inside was a loosely rolled scroll of paper that had expanded to nearly fill the entire container. Junior pulled the paper from the box. He took it gingerly by one end and slowly let it unwind. The whole thing was enormous and held together with tape. It was uneven and patchwork and immense in its scope.

"What is this, mom?"

"Hopefully one of my greatest achievement: my family tree."

Junior moved the box off the table and used the space to roll out as much of the document as possible. It dropped off both the end of the table. Junior moved to the left side of the tree and found it: the trunk of the tree. He bent over and scrutinized it like a rare diamond. The names of family members were written in careful calligraphy and framed in ornate black rectangles. They were full names, sometimes breaking into several lines. Below the frame were two columns of text: birth date and place on one side; death date and place on the other. Between the two was an ornamental dash, undulating like the lilting path from life to death. Questions marks stood in for these missing details. Some birth and death places were jotted with "(likely)."

Junior noticed that some of the relatives had two-digit codes jotted next to them.

"What are these numbers here?"

"You'll see later."

"Okay…"

As Junior traced the genealogy closer and closer to now, images of people began to show up. Dozens of stony, unsmiling men and women stared up from the paper. Sometimes a pod of names surrounded a family portrait. Almost at the same time as the photographs, small slips of paper started showing up above the names.

"Signatures!"

"Yes."

"You got signatures?"

"Where possible."

"How?"

"Legal records. Government records, mostly. Contracts. Some from personal letters or cards."

"Wow, Mom. This is incredible." Junior kept going. The names began to get less and less obscure, but he still had only passing memories of their sounds. Until he got to one that stood out like a spotlight.

"Hey. It's your dad."

Junior found himself staring at the black-and-white portrait of Jacob Keller. He was a man in his mid-thirties or early forties. He sat upright against a dark, textured background like a statue. He wore a white, collared shirt, sleeves rolled up past the elbows. He wore a dark neck tie. His hair was dark and wavy at the sides and on top, like it was sculpted that way. He was clean shaven and unsmiling. His eyes were kind.

Junior expected a flowing, beautiful signature like his mother's handwriting. Instead, Jacob's signature was barely more than a wavy line. Two letters were discernible: J and K. The final "r" became a tail that stretched off the tiny rectangle and disappeared to somewhere infinitely.

"Where did you get your dad's signature?"

"From him. I asked him for it."

Junior looked up and squinted at his mother. "How long have you been working on this?"

"Since my first first pregnancy," Jane said. "Before you were born."

Jane looked away. Junior started. He opened his mouth to ask a dozen questions.

"I wanted my babies to know where they came from and who they came from."

Junior closed his mouth and frowned.

"Why didn't you tell us? If it's for us?"

"Oh, I did. I'm sure you've seen it. When you all were younger. Probably before Lillian. Maybe Rebecca. But… I stopped working on it."

"Why did you stop working on it?"

"My collaborator died in 1953. It was hard to go on after that."

"Uncle Jack was helping you with this? Did he do a Becker tree, too?"

"He did a small tree for the Beckers. He didn't get around to finishing it. Not sure where he would have put it, either."

Junior roamed the scroll with his eyes. He caught sight of a familiar portrait.

"Hey, it's-"

"Help me roll this back up, Junior, before it comes apart. I'm just so nervous about losing all this hard work."

Junior felt disappointment tuck at him, but he began to roll it slowly, gently. When it was a cylinder again, Junior tucked it under his arm.

"I assume you want to take it home."

"Yes, please."

Jane's eyes were a little sadder for the walk down memory lane. They put the lid back on the box and locked it and pushed a button by the door. Jennifer returned with the guards and picked up the box. She walked them back to the front where they signed out. Jennifer thanked them so much for coming by.

"Jane," Jennifer said, "you look a little sad. Do you need a hug?"

Jane began to make a face but stopped herself.

"That would be nice."

Jennifer raced around the desk and gave Jane a hug. Jane thought it was a rather nice hug.

"Good-bye, Jennifer," Jane said.

"See you later," Jennifer said.

A letter from President Josiah Bartlett to Jane. Dated April 10, 1951.
—

President Josiah Bartlett
102 S Pennsylvania Ave.
Suite 100
Meridian University
Meridian, SD 57116

Ms. Keller,

As president of Meridian University, it is my duty to see to the safety and security of each and every one of my students. These threats are often from off-campus actors, and I am able to shield most of our students from them. I take my job very seriously, and I take every complaint and threat very seriously. I grow very alarmed when troublemakers appear to be stirred up in our midst.

I am writing you in the wake of some serious accusations that authorities and your fellow students have made. I've heard that you intend to incite a riot at the War & Peace Protest on Thursday. I have not had a chance to confer with the organizers of that protest, but I have asked and they have assured me that it will be a peaceful and thoughtful protest. If there's a chance of violence, I cannot allow the protest to continue.

I've read your poetry Ms. Keller, and there is no doubt that you have a great talent. However, your words are incendiary. You must see that. That kind of power is dangerous, especially in these chaotic and dangerous times. Words can be taken back or hidden away, but actions cannot. If your poetry causes harm to a fellow student, could you really live with yourself?

I know that you have loved ones fighting in the war, and that you probably feel a great deal of stress and sadness and loneliness. War can be especially hard on the women left behind. I encourage all our students to take the time they need to to adjust to these circumstances. We have counselors on campus that are willing and able to speak with you at any time to discuss your feelings.

These are difficult times, Ms. Keller. College is a time of transition for all students, and some adjust to it better than others. It is a time when students must decide the path their lives will take. It is a time for deciding what kind of person one will be. It is also a time when students are susceptible and easily manipulated. Take extreme care that you are not taking advantage of this fact in your fellow classmates.

Just because a weak mind may be easily turned and molded by a stronger one does not mean that it should be so. In fact, the stronger mind should protect the weaker ones. I trust you take my meaning.

My desire with this letter is to get your agreement not to attend the War & Peace Protest. Your failure to comply with the wishes of this office may result in a complete expulsion from the Meridian University. Any indication of malfeasance would go onto your official transcript. This is a very serious situation, Ms. Keller. I hope you thoughtfully consider the consequences before acting.

Sincerely,
President Bartlett

Junior started heading home, but Jane began to redirect him as soon as the skyscrapers took their rest. When he should have turned right, she asked him to turn left. They followed Lower Lake Street to where the lake gave way to swamp which then gave way to solid ground and house after house. Just before the railroad tracks, she told him to turn right. They took a rather steep hill lined with thick trees and came out onto a broad avenue at the top. They drove past St. Thomas Aquinas, curved back and headed out of town.

"Oh, I see what's happening here. You showed me the family goods, and now you're going send me to sleep with the… worms."

The road they were on intersected with Highway 34. Jane sent them right.

"Are we going back out to Beck's?"

They drove on in silence.

"Turn left," Jane said as they neared a fenced plot of land buttressed by corn fields. Junior turned into the driveway and drove forward as far in as he could get before reaching the gate. He jumped out and ran over. The gate wasn't locked, so he was able to lift the guard. Junior opened the gate as wide as it went. He slowly drove into the Catholic cemetery. Jane didn't have to direct him from here.

"I'll need help getting out," Jane said, "but I want to be alone."

Junior nodded. He parked as close as he could and got out. They performed their ritual, and Jane walked herself around the car. She negotiated climb onto the grass and found herself standing at John's grave. Junior got back in the car and busied himself with his phone.

Jane stared at the marker a long time without saying or thinking anything.

"You probably know by now," she said to the headstone. "I hope you also know that I never wanted to hurt you. That I always loved you."

The headstone was an iridescent color. It was bright blue, like the sky in summer, and it was specked with ovals of something that looked like pearl. John had been in love with the color for a long time. When he got sick, he insisted on it.

"I hate this color," Jane said. "But you know that, too."

"You can be proud of your kids. They've been good to me for a very, very long time. Especially Lillian. She's as much a mom to me as I was to her. You were right about her. You were always right. I think of you every day, John, but now I'll really get to see you. I've lived so much of my life without you. More than with you. Yet, I feel you and see you every single day. It's amazing how you left your mark on all of us. Even Lillian, who was only six. She frowns at me the same way you used to, when I'm being stubborn. Which is always."

Jane suddenly wished she had flowers to leave, but she had nothing. She reached into her pockets for something. She found a packet of sugar from the diner. Jane leaned over and rested the sugar packet on the granite.

"Something for your coffee. You still love coffee, don't you?"

"You'll have a spot for me, right? I might not get there right away. I… I had confession today, but a day of memories like this brings to mind all sorts of things… I suppose I had my whole life to confess that stuff, and I was busy with other things. With children and fighting and stories."

Jane felt her legs getting tired. They started to tremble, and her body started to shake. Junior's door opened.

"Need help mom?"

"Yeah…" Jane called out. "Getting worn out."

Junior hopped out and helped guide her back to her seat. When she was in position, Junior got back in and started the vehicle.

"Did you say what you wanted to say?"

"No," Jane said thoughtfully. "I said what I had to say. I wanted to say so much more."

"We can stay."

"No."

"Are you-"

"Home," said Jane. "Take me home. I need a nap, and you have supper to finish."

Junior put the car in drive. Jane watched the gravestone as they pulled away. Even on an overcast day, the pearl ovals winked a little. They rounded the corner, and the grave twinkled out of sight.

A letter from John Becker, Sr., to Jane. Dated November 28, 1950.
—

Blue J:

I've kept all your letters. They line a space between my bunk and the wall. The envelopes are so similar, I had to date them to keep track. Your latest letter is no different on the outside. It matches the rest in nearly every way: white paper, neat address, same stamps in the corner. But you drew two hearts below the "Becker" in my name. I didn't know what it meant for the longest time.

How are you feeling? You didn't say much about that. Are you hurt? Your letter was more or less a sober list of facts. I know you, Janey, and I know more churns below the surface. There are things you would certainly tell me in person. Why can't you put them to paper when I'm so far away? Tell me a story, Janey.

I'll fill in the blanks. You're writing these letters from your dad's office. It's cosy, away from your family. You can think and focus and take your time. You're probably using that ancient rolling desk of his.

I don't get such an ideal writing spot. I'm on my bunk jotting notes by the light of a single flashlight. I have to tuck it under my chin. It's hard to focus on my letters. Every little sound out there puts me on edge. Some of the guys have nightmares, and I lose my pen every time.

You cried on your letter. I could see the little stains. The ink ran a little. I know you're not as fine as you say you are. I don't know why you won't tell me more. Maybe you don't want to distract me, but I'm distracted anyway. I'm distracted when everything's perfect back home, because I want to be back home.

You're right, though. I'm awfully distracted. Other fellas have to yell at me two or three times just to get my attention. I don't have anyone to talk to about this, either. Most of these fellas are young. No wife. Maybe no girlfriend. Nothing steady. No one else was trying to build a life before they got swept away.

A name came to me. I want you to consider it: Grace. I was saying a rosary for you and the baby, and "Full of grace" just popped into my head. I couldn't get off that line. Couldn't say the rest of the prayer. I had to stop entirely and just head back to bunk, because I thought something was wrong with my brain. But maybe God was telling me that her name is Grace and that she's up there with him, waiting for us. Anyway, think about it.

Dearest, deepest love,
John

Lily was waiting for them when they returned home. She was sitting at the kitchen table doing on school work. She looked tired and stretched, and she smiled meekly when they came in.

"I was starting to think I needed to send out a search party," she told them as they walked in.

"Good," said Junior. "She kept trying to kill me. Thankfully, I've been working out, so I could defend myself."

Jane rolled her eyes. Lily helped Jane remove her coat and shoes. Jane could barely stand for it. She felt her legs threatening to give up. She started to shuffle into the living room. She felt weaker and weaker, and her side was enraged.

"What do you want to do, mom?" Lily asked.

Jane wanted to answer, but it took all her focus and energy to keep walking.

"She said she was ready for a nap," Junior told Lily. "It's been a long afternoon. It's nearly four, mom."

Jane said nothing. She could only think about her steps, one after one after one in the direction of her chair. Lily was at her side, guiding her in and holding the chair steady. They got her seated but she hit the seat hard. She had no energy left to push back against gravity. Lily put the walker aside and reclined the chair. Junior found some blankets.

"Here you go, mom," he said, draping it over her tiny, shivering body.

The blanket felt like nothing. Jane couldn't get any warmth into her body. Her body was ready to stop being a body.

"Cold, mom?"

Jane tried to nod. Lily grabbed another blanket and tossed it on. Jane felt the heaviness of the blankets, but they didn't seem to bring her any warmth. It was like being wrapped in death. She opened her mouth to say something but nothing came out.

"Good, mom?"

Jane wasn't good. She felt panic starting to rise. She couldn't move. She couldn't talk. Lily was smiling at her, but Jane was miles away under those blankets, floating through space. The pain flared up, like fire licking at her side. The image of it reminded her of something from her childhood. She wanted something for the pain. She tried to ask, to move her mouth, but her body wasn't listening to her.

"You just call if you need anything," Lily said, and she left the room. They both left the room. Jane felt their energy leave her, and she felt further away than ever.

Jane wanted to scream. She wanted to throw the covers off. She wanted to stay here. These were people she loved, people she'd created out of love. She wasn't ready to be without them. She hadn't seen everyone. She hadn't talked to everyone. She wasn't finished.

Jane hands were on her lap, and she felt her pockets. She remembered what was in those pockets. She hadn't passed it on, just like she hadn't passed on so many things. A flood of unwritten letters and unspoken words came to Jane in her stupor. She felt drowned by them. They made her eyes tired. They made her eyes heavy. Her body was void, and her side was fire. Jane fought and fought and fought, but the darkness came for her.

And Jane closed her eyes.

Chapter 5

Junior sat with his mother in an idling car in front of St. Thomas Aquinas Church in Stone City. He tapped a rhythm on the steering wheel to a song the neither he nor she could hear. He was trying to seem nonchalant.

"Where to, mom? Back home? I could set you up with a movie or some books. To the cemetery? You could visit your grave," John, Jr., laughed. "Or dad's."

"No, I'll be seeing him soon enough."

"Look, mom-"

"What time is it?"

"It's 9:44."

"Take me to the cafe. The girls will still be there."

"Mom, maybe we should-"

"Let's go, John."

John chewed on his lower lip. "Sure. Sounds good," he said, and put the car in reverse. He headed north to the Hilltop Cafe that overlooked the city. Jane was quiet, but Junior fidgeted and shifted as he drove.

"What's wrong, son?"

"Lily said you're going to kill yourself today."

"That's not what I said."

"Lily told me-"

"I said I'm going to die today. Those are not the same thing."

"Okay, well, the end result is still pretty sad for me. I mean… you're my mom."

"And you're my eldest."

"You mispronounced "favorite," but that's fine. You're getting old."

Jane smiled. The pastoral suburb of Stone City passed by their windows.

"You're not that old, mom."

"I know. I'm not that young, either."

"What makes you think you're going to die today? Do you feel okay?"

"I feel well enough."

"Have you talked to Rose? She's a doctor, you know. Free medical advice."

"Gracious, Junior. I'm not terminal. It's just... everyone dies."

"Is that how it goes? People just decide when their last day is?"

"No, that's not how it goes."

"Choose tomorrow. Give us some time to put things into order. Jake and Rose can make a flight tonight. They can't make it flight today."

"I didn't choose today, Junior. Today chose me."

"Is that how it works?"

"That's how it worked for your father."

The mood shifted. It was quiet in the car suddenly. They drove through the streets of town, and Jane watched out her window at the blocks of buildings old and new, changes and eternal, fading and glowing. Some had been there as long as she had, or longer. Their facades seemed antique to her now.

"How was mass?"

"It was fine."

Jane offered nothing else. They began to climb the hill.

"Mom." Junior put a hand on Jane's shoulder. "You know I'd do anything for you."

Jane turned to him. She smiled and her eyes shone a little.

"You have, Junior. And I thank you for that. It hasn't been an easy life for us, but it has been blessed."

"It's not quite over, you know."

"No. Not yet."

"How does that Bible verse go? None of us can know the day-"

"Don't you go quoting scripture to me, Johnathon Jacob Becker, Jr."

John grimaced. "Eeesh. All three names and the suffix."

They crested the hill, and Jane could look out over the town of her lifetime. There were so many nooks that she could read like a book. Spotted along them were patches of the new and unfamiliar. The town was changing as it always had. Jane knew from an early age that nothing in life is permanent, least of all the artificial things people build upon the natural things God built.

Junior pulled into the gravel parking lot of the cafe and found a spot close to the front door. He helped Jane into the cafe, and they quickly found Jane's circle. It was a fleet of white-haired, garrulous old women in the midst of an animated conversation. Coffee mugs dotted the tabletop as did little used packets of sugar and thumb-sized tubs of creamer.

"Jane!" they shouted.

"So lovely to see you!"

"You made it! The circle is complete."

"Jane, dear, don't stress yourself. We'll come to you."

"Hello."

One of the women came forward to help with Jane's walker and chair. She and Junior set Jane gently onto the padded wooden chair. Junior scooted her in. Jane smiled at the other ladies who were immediately drawn to her. The closest ones put a hand on Jane's hand or arm or shoulder. Jane felt warm.

When the waitress walked by, John asked for a cup of coffee for Jane. He remained there until it was brought out. Then he bent over to look his mom in the eyes.

"Need anything else, Mom?"

Jane shook her head, "No."

"Okay. When should I be back?"

"Oh, we won't be here that long."

"Two hours," threw in one of the women. "If you're lucky."

John laughed.

"Two hours it is. Enjoy your coffee, ladies. Try not to fall in love with me."

The ladies chuckled, but he was already a memory to them.

A letter from John Becker, Sr., to Jane. Dated January 8, 1952.
—

Blue J:

You can probably tell from the letterhead that I'm writing you from a military hospital. Needless to say, my service to my country has not been uneventful.

About two weeks ago, I was on a routine perimeter check with a couple other guys in the company. They tell me (because I don't remember) that I started talking nonsense. They were normal words but they weren't coming out in normal ways. Then I started to wander away. They tried to redirect me, but I kept on insisting on walking the way I was going, which was out toward nowhere.

They had to restrain me and transport me back to the medic. The medic didn't like what he saw, and I was transported to this hospital. The trip to the hospital is really the first thing I remember. I didn't have any idea what was going on, but I was making sense again, so they felt a little better about things.

They gave me some exams at the hospital. Everything checked out fine. Something strange had happened, but they couldn't quite pin down what. They gave me some antibiotics thinking maybe I had a blood infection or venereal disease. (I absolutely do not have a venereal disease.) Then they sent me back with orders to be under observation.

Everything was fine until this week. A couple days ago, we were marching through the jungle when I lost vision in my right eye and control of the right side of my body. I began listing to the right and walked right into a tree. My right arm wouldn't move and my leg got weak. They sent me immediately back to the hospital. They took a scan of my brain and found a series of tumors on my brain.

I'll just come out with it: they say I have cancer, Janey.

I was informed today that I'm going to get a medical discharge and sent home. I'm not entirely sure how I feel about that. They tell me this tumor is nothing to mess with. The doctors were grim but hopeful. They've already sent details and scans to Dr. Bushnell. He may have already talked to you about this.

I didn't write earlier because I didn't want to worry you for no reason. I'm writing now because now there's a reason. It sounds like they can do some intensive treatments that will give me a fighting chance, but brain cancer, especially the kind I have, is nasty stuff. The doctor called it a Medusa cancer that just burrows in and when you cut its head off it seems to grow three more. The doctor has also seen many patients make a full recovery and live out long, blissful lives. I promise that'll be us.

Don't tell the kids just yet. You can tell them that I'm coming home early. If they ask why, tell them that dad will tell them about it when he gets home. Junior and Jake will probably have lots of questions, but I want to be the one to deal with it. I want to show them how fine I am, and you shouldn't have to take on even more than you have to.

I love you. I love you. I love you. And I'll see you soon.

Dearest, deepest love,

John

John, Jr., sat in his car in the driveway of his mom's house with a bag of groceries haphazardly settled on the passenger seat near him. In his cupholder was a travel mug. He pulled off the lid and checked the level. Then he unscrewed the lid on the Crown Royal and tipped a couple of ounces into the mug. Through the big picture windows in the dining room, Junior could see his brother, James, appear and disappear, watching something far behind Junior. Junior took a sip of his drink and added another shot of Crown to it.

A stone had settled in Junior's stomach ever since Lily's phone call that morning. It was dense and unrelenting. His mother seemed fine to him, but the stone didn't melt away. Watching Jane make amends and settle scores coated the stone with granite layers. Each sip of Crown and diet cola washed a little of it away.

He was proud of himself for thinking of supper. The gathering would work in either scenario. If this really was her last day on Earth, then supper would be one last big family gathering. If it was all in her head, then supper might be just what she needs to snap out of it. His phone rang.

"Hello, dear," he said.

"How are you doing?" Hillary asked.

"Well, I waited until I was done driving to start drinking, so that's something."

"Uh oh. Are you-"

"I'm fine. Just something to take the edge off. I'll be fine to drive in twenty minutes."

Junior could hear his wife thinking on the other end.

"Should I come over? I could help out or drive you around or whatever else."

"No, it'll be fine. James is here. There are things he can do to help."

"It's just…"

Junior felt himself getting annoyed.

"What? I can't have a drink now?"

"In the middle of the day?"

"I'm an adult."

"It just reminds me of when it was like this all the time. And I would get calls from-"

"I know."

"And it just about ruined-"

"I know! I know. I know…"

Junior's finger had been tracing the lid of the travel mug. It caught in the mouth.

"Okay, well, just let me know how I can help."

"I will. Say, did I tell you about supper?"

"I don't think so."

"Supper at mom's. A big family gathering kind of thing."

"A last supper?"

"I like to think of it as a come-to-your-senses supper."

"Can I bring anything?"

"Well," Junior rustled through the grocery bags in the passenger seat. "I have most things covered. You could bring rolls. Or a fruit salad maybe."

"I'll do a fruit salad. That sounds good."

"Okay. Sounds good."

"What time?"

"Six."

"Okay. I'll be over before then. Love you. Bye."

"Love you, too."

Junior ended the phone call and checked the time. It was 1:30. He grabbed the grocery bag from the passenger seat and opened the car drop. He decided to leave the travel mug and whisky in the vehicle. If he needed them later, he knew where they'd be waiting.

A letter from Jack Becker to Jane. Dated March 30, 1952.
—

Janey Janey:

Be sure you're alone before reading this letter. Maybe that goes without saying.

Janey, I can't banish you from my thoughts. I try. I fail. Janey Janey, the twice woman of my dreams. My days with Ethel are ever darker. I long in my heart to tell her the truth about us. Not to hurt her, but to give her the chance to love someone else. She's wasting her love on me, and she has so much of it. Every year that passes with the unspoken truth amplifies the pain she'll feel when it finds voice.

I know it's not the same for you. You've said as much to me many times. You love us both. How a person can live such two distinct realities simultaneously is either a gift or a curse. Knowing in my heart that my love for Ethel is a shallow facsimile of the love I have for you, I cannot laugh at her jokes or smile at her witty statements or fawn over her.

I can't stop this passion for you. I dream of the soft cream of your skin, the silk of your lips. Your gentle touch on my cheek starts in me an electricity. I sometimes hear your voice in the birds outside our home. They sing in a way that I've heard you sing. Did they learn that song from you?

I sit and watch them and sigh, and Ethel clucks her tongue at me. I fear she might be catching on to me. She sighs heavily when we sit together in the quiet. I don't know if she wants something from me or to say something or if it's nothing at all. You are the only person I know could gather such information from her, but I dare not ask you.

When I can't sleep, I remember the family tree. I remember the fervent and gasping need we had for each other in that small lake cabin. And I hear that you're expecting again. Congratulations. I can't help but wonder at the timing.

Enough of that. I'll only go mad with the thought of it. You talk about the fire in my eyes, but that fire is just a reflection of you and my passion for you. I can't stand the thought of sharing you with anyone, not even my brother. Those thoughts come at me sometimes, dark and quick like shadows with teeth. They pull me down into the bottom of a bottle, and I wake up days later in harsh sunlight. It isn't your fault. These shadows have long preyed on me.

I'm sorry. I'll stop.

How are you coming with finding your father's father's signature? I remember it was eluding you. I had a wild thought on those lines: business contracts. He was a successful farmer, wasn't he? You could check the records of general stores in the surrounding towns. I also wondered whether birth certificates might be a good way of getting parental signatures. I plan to test my theory on that with Ethel's birth certificate. It would be nothing to get her permission to request it.

Inspired by your work, I've begun a Becker Family Tree. Our records are less consistent, it appears. I haven't been able to reach as far back as you, but I am well on my way to collecting the portraits and signatures. I've gotten my parents, my grandfather, my great-grandmother and several cousins and uncles. I will need John's signature at some point. It might be a good opportunity for me to pay you a visit. I wouldn't stay long. I just want to be near you.

Let me hear from you with all possible haste. Gaps between letters are a grave for me. I drink and wait, eager to see your handwriting upon an envelope. Perhaps you should write to Ethel, too. She is very curious about all our letters.

Yours in life and love,
Jumping Jack Flash

John, Jr., sat in his car on an outer road of the St. Thomas Aquinas Catholic Cemetery. Two tires rested on grass, two on gravel, as he stared through the windshield at nothing. In his cupholder was the travel mug, again. It had been full of Crown Royal and diet soda, but it was nearly empty. Junior took a sip and opened the driver side door. He climbed out, travel mug in hand, and shut the door behind him. His mother's grave was ten spaces away. His father's rested beside her.

There was a rectangle of fresh dirt marking Jane's tombstone. It would take a while for seed to grow. Eventually, grass would overtake her plot and make it look seamless with the broader cemetery. For now, it was just brown dirt.

"I've been reading your letters," Junior said. "I know you wanted them gone, but I convinced Lily that we should go through them first. Don't worry. Lily's on vacation, so she doesn't know. I read some interesting things, mom."

Junior took a sip.

"I found some letters from Uncle Jack that seemed pretty uncommon. Maybe inappropriate. I don't know everything that he's talking about, but some of them paint a pretty strong picture. I sure hope everything was mutual."

Junior reached into his back pocket and pulled out a yellowed rectangle of paper. He unfolded it and looked at it for a while.

"He was pretty wound up, mom. He was so in love with you, it was... hard to read, actually. Hard to think about. And poor Aunt Ethel..."

Junior jabbed a finger at a line near the top of the letter.

"The date. The date he wrote this. It's really... really... telling. You probably know that. You probably know exactly what I'm talking about. Any comment? Any witty response? What do you have to say for yourself?"

The only sound was the wind blowing through the fir trees.

"Did you kill Uncle Jack, mom?"

Junior waited for a response but got nothing. He folded the paper back up. He took another sip.

"You were one person, but you were two entirely different people, mom. I always thought you were my hero. But here you were, getting what you wanted out of people and giving nothing back unless you had to. With Jake. With Rose. With all of us. You show people whatever part of you is necessary to get what you want. Is that it?"

Junior kneeled on the ground. He rolled the paper into a tight cylinder. He stared at the stone and noticed a sugar packet resting on the granite.

"You must have taught me well. Hillary tells me all the time now that there's two of me: one when I drink, and one when I don't. And she says, "I'm thinking of divorcing one of them." That's what she says. She says it's like a switch, and she hates it. Hates me for it. And then I found those letters, and I stopped wondering where I got it from."

Junior shoved the cylinder into the ground. He pushed with all his might so that the paper would disappear into the dirt and become dirt itself. He wanted those anguished words to disappear and become something else. Something useful.

"I can't be two people anymore, mom. I can't live two lives."

Junior unscrewed the lid to his travel mug. He held it out and upturned the mug. The whisky caught the wind and splashed against his legs, wetting his pants and shoes. He replaced the lid. Then Junior walked back to his car and drove slowly and carefully home.

A letter from Jane Becker to John, Jr. Undated.
—

John, Junior:

When you read this, I'll be dead. As the hours wind down, I'm making a concerted effort to tie up loose ends and pass on the things that I think my children would appreciate the most. As my eldest and most dependable son, I leave for you a two things.

You have seen the family history. You seemed as touched by it as I was when in the fits of passion. I had had someone else in mind, but I knew then that it would go best to you. I want you to update it and improve it, but I want you to do something else. I want you to display it. Don't hide it away like I did. Don't make it a secret. Make it a living document, just as the family is living.

The other thing I have for you is a task. There is a box in the basement in the unfinished storage room, the room I forbade you children from playing in. Inside that box are pages and pages of writings. Some of them are letters to me. Others are manuscripts and works of my own writing. I want you to destroy my letters.

Some of my own writing has been promised to your siblings, but there is much of it that has no home. If you enjoy what you read, you are free to keep it and do whatever with it. If you don't, then you may destroy it. It does no one any good now, least of all me. You'll find poetry, non-fiction and even some novels. I won't say they are worth publication. They certainly weren't back then. The forces I ran up against assured me that I had no story to tell. Not in my own words, at least.

The letters are not to be read or kept. I trust that you'll follow my wishes on this. Gather them together and burn them. I don't want them thrown out or torn up. Turn my letters into heat and smoke, John, and watch them float away. The import of them is over and done with. The letters should be given over to peace and release.

I know you'll be okay. I don't have to hold your hand like some of the others. And I know you'll fulfill my wishes. I trust no one more.

Love forever and always,
Your mother,
Jane Becker

Chapter 6

The area where Jacob Becker did most of his painting was a glorified crawl space in the attic of his house. The windows were nearly always wide open, even in November, because the space had no ventilation. Jacob often painted wearing his winter jacket and gloves with the fingertips cut off. This time of year, he could see his breath. He shivered as he painted, and it made frantic, uneven streaks across the canvas.

Jake stepped back from the canvas and surveyed it. He grabbed a reference photo from the table and held it up so that both images were in his sight. The image was a photo of his daughter, smiling under a tree in their backyard. The painting was her face on a nearly monstrous scale. The canvas was nearly as tall as the girl.

But it was wrong. It looked ugly and lifeless to Jake. The strokes weren't coming together. They remained stubbornly separate streaks of paint. He tossed the photograph onto the table and ran his hands through his hair. He was surrounded by similar such portraits. His other daughter, his wife, friends, strangers, all done in the same frozen crawl space, with the same thick paint, with the same shivering hands. Those felt inspired. This felt insipid. He was suffering art block.

There was a knock on the door frame behind him.

"How's the painting going?"

The voice belonged to Amy, Jake's wife. She was petite and lean with long blond hair pulled into a pony tail. She had on an old, stained t-shirt and baggy jeans. She leaned on the door jamb and crossed her arms over her chest. Jake reached forward and pulled the canvas off the easel. He showed her his disaster.

"Oh... that's... unsettling."

"So it's not just me?"

Jake dropped the canvas to the floor and leaned it against his desk.

"It just looks sorta... life-less?"

"Yeah." Jake pulled his gloves off and held them together. He slapped the desk with them. "Dead. Hollow. Empty."

"How many portraits do you have left?"

"Two."

"That's not bad. How much time do you have to paint them?"

"The gallery opens in three weeks, but they want all the pieces in two weeks, and I should probably be done painting in one week."

"Is that..."

"Possible. But uncomfortable."

Jake picked up the canvas and carried it across the room to another table. He started to wash off his work. To start fresh.

"How's your painting going?" Jake asked his wife.

"Well, it's a lot darker than I thought it would be," Amy said, picking at splotches of paint on her palm, "but I think it'll look nice. It'll still brighten up that hallway."

"It needs it, that's for sure."

"I considered a second coat, but I don't-"

"Uh huh..."

Jake was lost to the process of stripping the canvas. Amy wavered in the doorway for a moment before leaving to return to her own work. When Jake finally cleaned the canvas, he set it back on the easel and looked at the photograph. He held it close to his face and studied the image. It wasn't moving him. He tried to follow the lines and find inspiration. He tried to study the contrast and uncover a puzzle. He tried to discover an unfamiliar color tucked into the picture.

He lay the photo on the desk and went to his wall of colors. It was truly a tool shelf, but the long, narrow plastic drawers fit his paint tubes perfectly. He closed his eyes and flung his arm at the wall until his fingers caught a handle. He pulled the drawer open and lifted the tube out.

"Cardinal Red," he said. "Can you believe- Honey?"

Jake was alone with his nostalgia. He went to the bookshelf in his studio and grabbed a thick book with a black spine. The title was "Birds of Central South Dakota," and he flipped to a well-worn page documenting the Northern Cardinal. The brilliance of the bird in the photograph nearly took his breath away.

Jake's phone rang.

A letter from Jacob Becker to Jane. Dated August 30, 1969.
—

Hi Mom!

First of all, the university is gorgeous. I know you weren't excited to drop me off last month, but I think you would really dig this place. There's nature everywhere. It's like the buildings grew out of the forest. The buildings just sprouted out here. Everything jives so well together.

My classes are good. Undergrad was a breeze compared to grad school, but I'm really digging the classes. The professors treat you differently in the graduate classes. It's like they finally decide to take us seriously. Who am I kidding? We were awful as undergraduates. We got what we deserved.

Classes are tough but doable. I'm learning so much more about human form and the shapes that make up things in life. It's funny how I thought I had things all figured out when I graduated, and then this MFA program slapped me in the face. I learned pretty quickly that I didn't know half of what I thought I did. I'm really going to have to buckle down to survive this. You guys taught me to work hard, so I know I can do it.

I got a job the other day. I'm working at Chicken Parts. It's a fried chicken restaurant. There aren't any back home. I think it's a regional franchise. Everyone in the program told me not to get a job, but I need the money. We'll see how long I hold it down. I've already seen three employees quit and get replaced, so I think they're built for that kind of churn. They won't be too bummed to see me leave.

The house is pretty awesome. You met two of my roommates. The third one moved in after you left. All four of us are in different graduate programs. One other guy is getting a fine art MFA. The other two are in the math or computer science programs. We are all pretty nerdy but also pretty chill. We talk about Lord of the Rings all the time, and I couldn't be happier. We started playing a game called Dungeons and Dragons, which is like pretending to be a Tolkien character. You can cut the heads off goblins and cast magic spells. It's awesome. I wonder if I can find a way to work my nerdy or birdy interests into my art.

I guess life is pretty great right now. I mean, school is going to suck, but life will be good besides. I've been thinking a lot about what Christmas and summer is going to be like. I haven't made any plans, but I'm thinking about staying out here. I'll already have my room at the house, so I won't need to get housing. I'll have a job, so I can use that to rake in as much dough as possible. It would put less strain on you and the fam. One less mouth to feed. Less laundry to do. I don't want to be a drain.

I'll write again or call when I make up my mind. I still want to see you guys. I just don't know for how long or when.

I hope everything there is going well.

Love and peace,

Jacob

"Did you get something to eat at the cafe, mom?" John, Jr., asked.

Jane remembered only coffee and shook her head. She was secured in the vehicle and watching the landscape plod by.

"Want me to pick something up for you? I can make you something at home, or we can pick something up."

The chat with the girls had put some pep into her, stirred some life back into her. Jane was hungry.

"Chinese food," she said.

"Can you have that? Aren't you supposed to watch your sodium?"

"Not today, John."

Junior bit the inside of his cheek but didn't say anything. He headed toward the only Chinese food restaurant in town. It was owned by a Vietnamese family named the Trans. They knew Jane and her order by heart: orange chicken with half the rice and twice the veggies. As Junior pulled onto main street, his phone began to ring. He brought it up and into his eye line.

"It's Jake, and I doubt he's calling about the Trojans."

Junior answered it, exchanged pleasantries and handed the phone to Jane.

"Hi, mom. It's Jake."

Jane had always thought that Jake's voice sounded like a wave. It was smooth. It had a secret energy that snaked under its surface. It was nice to hear his voice.

"How are you?"

"Oh… I'm surviving." She laughed lightly.

"Yeah… Lily told us. How, uh… how… what's going on?"

"Nothing much. Just got done with mass and coffee and now John is picking up lunch."

Junior pulled up to the Fat Panda and parked the car.

"Same old?" he asked.

Jane nodded, and Junior went to place the order.

"That's not what I meant, mom. I mean, what's really going on?"

"Oh, nothing's going on. I can't really explain it. I just woke up knowing."

"Knowing what?"

"Something most people don't."

That was all she gave him. It was all should could give him.

"Well, okay… That's… pretty special, I suppose…"

Jane said nothing. She was content in silences.

"I don't know what to say, mom. I can't get there on short notice like this. I have these portraits-"

"I know, Jake. You'll be back next week, I'm sure."

"Mom. You mean for the funeral? That's really morbid."

"Jake, I'm at the end of my life. I'm past being precious about these things. There are too many other important things to do today."

"I suppose."

"You were always uncomfortable with death. It was hard on you."

"You mean… Yeah. It was tough. And I was in a transition from high school to college."

"And moved away."

"…and moved away. Did you ever?"

"Move away to college?"

"Yeah."

"Oh, sure. I went to college for a little while."

"But you didn't stay?"

"Oh, I stayed as long as I could," Jane smiled. "I was too much trouble for them."

Jake laughed. "That doesn't surprise me."

"And your father was fighting in Korea, and that was hard. I moved home to be with my family. To wait for him."

Jane saw a flash of red pass by her window. She followed it through the windshield and watched it light on a leaf-bare tree in the parking lot. It was a cardinal, male. He was large for a cardinal and as bright red as lipstick.

Jane heard Jake sigh from the other side of the country.

"I wish I could be there with you."

"I know. This isn't convenient for anyone."

"Is there anything I can do?"

"You can remember me. You can remember bird watching."

"We were always the first ones up. I remember you and I would sit in the kitchen and watch the birds come. My favorites were cardinals."

Jane smiled. "You got that from me."

"I don't see many of them around here. But every time I do, I think of those mornings. Do they still hang out in the yard?"

"Oh, from time to time. There aren't as many around these days. I'm actually looking at one right now."

As if eavesdropping, the cardinal suddenly leapt off the branch and flew away. Jane watched it travel down the road, turn and disappear.

"Is there anything I can do, mom?"

"You can give your family my love."

"I will. I do. They love you, too, mom. I love you."

"I love you, too, Jake."

"I never moved out here to get away from you. Maybe it felt that way. I was chased out here, you know? Dad's ghost chased me out here. I had to get away. Then I found a girl and started a family. I didn't visit at first because I couldn't be around those places. When I was ready to be around those places, then I had a family, and… Anyway, it wasn't you."

Jane felt her chin shake a little.

"Anyway, I have to get back to it. I'm sure you have a full day. I love you, mom. I… I hope I get to talk to you tomorrow."

"I love you, too, Jake," Jane said.

The call disconnected, and Jane set the phone in the cupholder. Junior came out moments later with a grease-stained paper sack. He set it on the floor behind the driver's seat and climbed in.

"How did that go?"

"It went well," Jane said, her voice sturdier than she'd expected.

"If he hadn't called you, would you have called him?"

Jane said nothing. Junior put the car in reverse.

"You know, if you're serious about this last day on earth thing, you might have to get a little uncomfortable."

Junior pulled out of the parking spot and headed back to Jane's house. Jane wondered if she had Rose's number in her phone.

An excerpt from Orville Becker's "Birds of Central South Dakota." Published 1993.

—

One of my favorite South Dakota birds is the northern cardinal, known scientifically as *Cardinalis cardinalis*. I'm not alone in my affection for this brilliant red species. It is the state bird for: Illinois, Indiana, Kentucky, North Carolina, Ohio, Virginia, and West Virginia. It is also the mascot for dozens of high school, college and professional sports teams. Think of the St. Louis Cardinals or Ball State University in Muncie, Indiana. One look at the bird is enough to see why there is such fascination.

The northern cardinal is between eight and nine inches long with a wingspan of around twelve inches and weighing about one and a half ounces. This makes it a mid-sized songbird. It's large enough to get noticed but small enough to live in our backyards and forests easily. Northern cardinals make their homes in semi-open habitats like residential areas, clearings and parks. They are seed predators who take in insects and fruit to round out their diet. The ones that vacation in my backyard enjoy sunflower seeds, and I make sure a large bowl is available during the spring and summer seasons.

The northern cardinal enjoys a large migratory range. They live as far north as southern Canada, as far east as Maine, as far south as Florida, Texas and Mexico, and as far west as Texas. My home is on the western edge of the northern cardinal's habitat, but we see them frequently enough. I'm well known as a bird person, and I'm sure the bluejays have shared my reputation.

The female northern cardinal is tan and gray, often with splashes of red in her crest and across her back. Her beak is a faded red, almost an orange color in some cases. She blends beautifully with the woody brush and branches that she nests in. The male, on the other hand, is all about presentation. The male northern cardinal is bright red. The name and color actually come from the red worn by Roman Catholic cardinals in Rome. The red color is vibrant and bright across the chest, neck and crest. It deepens and darkens across the back, wings and tail. The beak is bright red, almost like a triangular piece of plastic. Surrounding the beak and eyes is a mask of black.

Northern cardinals are territorial birds. Males mark their turf with song. The songs are learned, not instinctive, and therefore they vary from region to region. This is one of my favorite details about cardinals. I wonder if others of their species appreciate how one member might adapt and change the songs it grew up hearing. Do cardinals do covers or remixes? Do they take requests? I hope one day to find out.

The ones that visit my house have a song that I've learned to listen for and mimic. It hasn't changed much in the decades that I've lived here, so I don't think new cardinals stray too far from the established song. I've tried to describe it to my son: *who-it, who-it; cherr-cherr-cherr-cherr-cherr*. Of course, this book is far too clumsy a medium to describe the beautiful melody they use. One must simply hear it to appreciate it.

Northern cardinals mate for life. They also stay together year-round. I find this spousal dedication interesting, if a bit unusual for such magnificent birds. It must be hard for the females to stay dedicated with so many beautiful males around. Then again, part of their courtship involves sharing a meal. The male will feed the female from what he has collected by passing it beak-to-beak. Cardinals sure do know how to do romance.

The portraits were already installed but each was covered by a gray curtain. There were ten portraits in all which made ten gray shrouds. Jake had commandeered a shrimp plate and three glasses of white wine.

"You are melting down. What is going on?" Amy asked, taking one of his wine flutes for herself. "That shrimp smells awful."

"You're insane," he tried to say through a mouth full of shrimp. The words came out in a gurgle, and some red cocktail sauce dribbled from the corner of Jake's mouth.

"Swallow. You have to give a speech in five minutes. Just relax. It'll go great. Your installations always do."

Jake watched as the gallery owner strolled into the center of the room. He clanged a spoon against his wine glass for attention. Jake's eyes froze on the man, and his mouth went dry. He reached for his wine, but Amy thrust a glass of water into his hand.

"Drink up," she said. "You'll thank me later."

Jake drank so quickly and so loudly that he didn't hear his name. In the awkward wait that followed, Amy gently pushed him toward the center of the room, sneaking the glass out of his hand at the same time. Jake trotted out to the gallery owner and took a short bow. He started back to his spot when the man put a hand on Jake's arm.

"Typical artist, hiding from the spotlight. Say a few words, won't you, Jake?"

His grip was tight. He thrust the microphone into Jake's hand and pulled Jake before him like a human shield. Jake cleared his throat into the mic.

"Uh, hello. My name is Jacob Becker. Welcome to my installation. Uh…"

He looked around the room at the dozens of faces he'd never seen before in his life hiding the six or seven he had. He found Amy's face in the crowd and took a deep breath.

"The title of this show is "Self Portrait of the Artist as a Crowd." I, uh, I got the idea when I started thinking of all people who come into an artist's life and make them the artist they are or the artist they turn into. I thought about how many painters do self portraits in moody lighting or exaggerate their best features or whatever. I decided to exaggerate the people in my life and paint a separate portrait for each of them. Some are family or friends. Some are collaborators. Some are alive. Some… And some are just inspirations, and they probably have no idea who I am. Or that I painted them. That's… that's kinda creepy actually. Anyway..."

Jake let the mic droop. He looked around the room for the owner who had slinked away during the speech. Jake shrugged.

"Unveil it?"

The owner nodded and motioned to one of the attendants. All the attendants walked to one of the covered portraits and gently removed the gray cloth. There was light clapping and then confusion. The portraits were larger than life. Each subject was cropped closely about the face and painted on large canvases. The effect was that every eyelash and pore and blemish was blindingly displayed. The paintings didn't just look real. They looked hyperreal. The colors and contrasts were exaggerated. Each canvas had the effect of giving each face a topographical appearance.

That wasn't what people were confused by. The second to last portrait in the line-up stood out from the rest. First was the color: cardinal red. Second was the subject: a male northern cardinal. Where every other portrait had been a human face, canvas 9 was bird.

Jake remained in the center of the room for a while. Then he floated back toward Amy and his shrimp plate and wine. He gorged himself with less vigor, the huge knot in his stomach having exorcised itself. He watched the patrons mill their circuit around the gallery. The cardinal drew the most attention and speculation. Some would search the crowd for Jake, and Jake would slowly turn to face the other way for a count of five.

When the crowd began to thin, Jake set his shrimp plate down.

"I'm going to go check on the cardinal," Jake told Amy.

"Check on it?"

"I mean, you know what I mean."

"It's okay to want to look at your own art."

"Ew. Don't be gross."

But he left anyway. Jake crossed the room in an awkward approximation of "nonchalance." The remaining patrons noticed his approach and cleared the way, sensing an unusual energy between the painting and its painter. When Jake got there, he noticed something awry. Next to every canvas was a small card on the wall that quoted a price for purchase. The cardinal had no card.

Jake looked around for the owner, hoping to flag him down. Amy came up behind Jake and put a hand on his shoulder.

"What's up?"

"Did you see this? They forgot the price card. I'm trying to flag down-"

"How do you feel about that?"

"Well…" Jake took a deep breath. "I mean, I'm not eager to sell it. It's not… It's not just a picture of a bird."

Amy feigned shock.

"You don't say."

Jake smiled wryly back.

"Yeah. It's like a deep personal statement and stuff. But I really struggled with whether to sell it or not, and… What's done is done. They need to do their job right. If you see-"

"I bought it." Jake stopped looking around and stared at his wife. Amy was smiling at him. "I put in an offer before the opening, because I knew how much it meant to you."

Jake's eyes glossed up. "You bought it? For me?"

"I did it for her. And for us. We can put it downstairs. It'll brighten up that hallway."

"She'd like that," Jake said, and he put his arm around Amy.

"So, you'll write me a check, or…"

A letter from Jane Becker to Jacob. Undated.
—

Dear Jacob:

When you read this, I'll be dead. As the hours wind down, I'm making a concerted effort to tie up loose ends and pass on the things that I think my children would appreciate the most. It will probably surprise you and the others that I'm a writer, although you won't see my name on any bookshelves or bestseller lists. You will, however, find at least one book with my words in it.

You definitely know that I've long had a fascination with birds. You and I sat for hours watching the birds in our yard, and I'm so happy to see that you picked up that interest as well. I know we didn't get to go out watching as much as you wanted to, but maybe I can make up for it now.

In my basement is an entire shelf of bird watching books. You'll find many volumes you already own, including the one I'm about to describe. It's called "Birds of Central South Dakota," and it's written by Orville Becker. Maybe you've wondered if the name "Becker" is coincidental or not. No, Orville is not a long lost relative of ours that you've never heard of. Orville is a pen name that I was asked to use when I published the book. I am Orville Becker.

Working on the book was a labor of love. I was inspired by our early morning sessions to put what I knew about birds into a book for others. I chose each species by watching our yard and then diving into research. I went into the forests with a camera and took every photo. I learned later that you're supposed to pitch nonfiction books to the publisher before you work on them. They may have a certain style or tone that you need to match. I didn't do that. Instead, I sent it around to dozens of publishers and received rejection after rejection. At last, I found one that was willing to read the manuscript and give comments.

They loved it, but they had doubts about being able to sell it. A woman with no formal education in ornithology seemed like a pretty difficult hurdle to clear, so they asked me to write under a pseudonym. Nothing else in the book would have to change. Just the name the cover. I was given a choice: to maintain my identity but never see my book published or to change my identity for the sake of seeing my project given a true life.

I chose life.

I don't regret that decision, but it's something that I think about a lot. The book never sold terribly well. I don't know if that was due to a lack of "credibility," like they said, or because they did a terrible job of marketing it. They never contacted me for a second edition, although I provided plenty of material for one.

Attached to this letter is a sheet of paper that explains the authenticity of my authorship and lists personal phone numbers to contact people at the publisher. I think the book needs a second edition cowritten by Jacob Becker. I'll call their office before you get this letter so that they know what's going to happen and that it's in keeping with my wishes. That is, if anyone there even remembers who I am.

Give my book a new life, Jacob. Be bold and uncompromising when I wasn't.

Love forever and always,
Your mother,
Jane Becker

Chapter 7

Rose Becker's phone was never on her person during the day. Lots of doctors carried theirs, the argument being it kept them connected to their nursing staff. Rose, however, felt it put more distance between her and her patients, so she kept it in her locker. When she went to her locker on her lunch break, she heard it chirping away. She recognized it as a voicemail alert.

The voicemail was from Lily. Lily sounded tense on the phone. It was about mom. Lily wondered if something medical could be at work, but Rose dismissed it. Confusion, mood swings, depression, these would be medical symptoms. This sounded like Jane being Jane.

"Dr. Becker, please report to nurses' station 2B."

Rose resolved to call Lily later and replaced the phone. She made her way out of the locker room and toward 2B. Rose had a slender but angular shape, like her brothers. She had a pretty face that wore a severe expression, cultivated from years of overcompensating as a woman doctor. She tried to soften her features for patients, but returned to her scowl when lost in thought. She nearly passed by the desk.

"Dr. Becker? Earth to Dr. Becker."

Rose stopped short and looked around for the familiar voice.

Rose smiled. "Nurse Tan, I assume this was urgent."

Leann Tan smiled back, but it quickly faded.

"Your sister called."

"She called you, too?"

"Probably when she couldn't get ahold of you."

They looked at each other. Rose looked at her watch.

"Well," said Rose. "I'll see you later."

"Hey," Leann frowned. "That's it?"

"I gotta go." Rose started back down the hallway.

"Did you call her back?"

"No."

"Are you ever?"

"I'm sure I will."

Rose was getting farther and farther away.

"We should talk about this."

"We'll talk later."

"This might be your last chance to talk to your mom."

"She's fine."

Leann had to raise her voice to reach Rose. Rose continued walking.

"I have lives to save!" Rose shouted. She turned the corner and headed toward the closest patient's room.

"Mr. Janes, how are you today?"

An older man with white hair looked up from his paper. "Just dandy, darlin'. Think I can go back to work soon?"

Rose pulled the clipboard of Jasper's chart out of its holder on the end of the bed. She checked the stats on the first and second pages.

"I don't know if I ever asked. What do you do for a living, Mr. Janes?"

"Oh," Jasper chuckled, "I'm just a button pusher."

"Where at?"

"Meridian Industries."

Rose looked up, and cocked her head to the side.

"Wait a minute. Jasper Janes of Meridian Industries?"

Jasper held his hands up. "Guilty."

"How much life insurance does your family get if I kill you off?"

Rose smirked at him.

"None, if it's murder, honey," he smirked back.

Rose dropped the chart back into the holder.

"White blood cell count is coming down, which is the primary thing I'm looking at. A day or two more, and you'll be right as rain."

Rose turned to leave.

"That's what I like to hear, sweetheart."

Rose stopped. She turned back.

"One more thing. I graduated top of my class, and I'm one heartbeat away from being chief of medicine. If you keep up this misogynistic nickname stuff, I'll order so many colonoscopies that you'll leave here feeling like a balloon."

She didn't even wait for his expression to change.

Leann found Rose in the break room. Rose was sprawled across the only couch in the room, flipping through the channels on the TV mounted high on the wall.

"Did you call her back?"

"Who?"

Leann went around the couch and tapped Rose on the forehead.

"Sit up."

Rose crunched up, and Leann plopped down on the couch. When Rose laid back, her head was in Leann's lap. Leann rested one arm on the back of the couch and the other cradled Rose's head.

"Let's talk," Leann said.

"I'm watching TV," Rose said, still flipping through the channels.

Leann snatched the remote from Rose's hand, hit the power button and tossed the remote across the room.

"Let's talk," she said again.

Rose groaned.

"You always want to talk."

"Did you call Lily back?"

Rose said nothing.

"If you don't call your mother today, you'll regret it."

"Why should I be the one to call her? Shouldn't she be apologizing to us?"

"Rose-"

"No, I mean it."

Rose sat up. She turned to face Leann. She took Leann's hands in hers.

"She turned her back on us. She abandoned us."

"She didn't-"

"She won't even let us visit."

Leann squeezed Rose's hands.

"Don't get upset. You're exaggerating."

"Like hell I am."

"Your mother didn't forbid us from visiting, she just doesn't want us to sleep in the same room."

"She's ashamed of us."

"She's just uncomfortable with a certain aspect of our relationship."

Rose pulled her hands away and stood up.

"Why are you defending her?"

Rose's voice was raising. Her hands were shaking.

"Seriously? I'm a Chinese lesbian, Rose. Sleeping in separate rooms is a small price to pay for being able to meet your family. You're exaggerating the-"

"Stop saying that."

Leann stopped. She took a breath.

"I don't want you to pass this energy onto your patients, so I'm stopping."

"Good," Rose said, oozing hostility.

"You should call your sister."

Rose groaned again. Leann stood and started to leave. Rose started to follow her.

"I'm not going to. She has to call me."

Leann left the break room and headed back toward nursing station 2B. Rose continued to follow.

"That old lady owes me an apology decades in the making. I'll be damned if-"

"Dr. Becker?"

Another nurse was there, apparating out of nowhere.

"Uh, yes?"

"Mr. Janes said that you had cleared him for discharge, but I didn't see any notes on his chart. I just wanted to double-check."

"Mr. Janes? He absolutely is not cleared for discharge."

Rose forgot her argument with Leann and blew past the nurse on her way to Jasper's room. When she charged in, he was nearly dressed.

"Sit your ass back down," Rose said.

"Dr. Becker?" the nurse exclaimed.

Jasper laughed.

"Well, well. Dr. Becker came to see me off."

"Where do you think you're going?"

"Well, sweetheart, you said my blood cells were going down, and I could leave in a couple days. Since I've always been an overachiever, I figure my blood cells would be down enough by now that I could still get some hours in at the office."

Rose grabbed his chart again, but there were no new blood test results on the paper.

"We haven't done your blood work since before I last saw you, so we don't know what your blood cells are doing. Until I give you the official word, you're not going anywhere."

"Well, sweetie-"

"And I can order security to have you restrained if I feel it's necessary."

"Dr. Becker..." the nurse standing next to Rose gave a low warning. Rose wheeled on her with a face red with fury. The nurse took a step back.

"Get back in your hospital gown, Mr. Janes, and bunker down for the night, because you just became my new project."

Jasper narrowed his eyes at Rose, but he remove the jacket he'd been in the process of donning.

"As you wish, Doctor."

"Nurse Gladstone, order a shallow colonoscopy for Mr. Janes. We want to make sure there's no sign of infection down there."

Jasper's eyebrows reached for the ceiling.

"I did what you asked, Dr. Becker," he said warningly.

"Not exactly," Rose said. "But you will. Sweetie."

Rose dropped the chart into its holder and left the room.

A poem by Jane Becker, published in the Meridian University Herald. Published 1951.
—
New America: 2 + 2 = 5

There is a cold spot in his room
    Where his body used to be.
    His spirit sags there
    Into a stain on the wood floor
    Split from the soul still his.

He holds a gun and shoots
    And the enemies shoot back
    And my heart goes pitter-pitter-pitter
    And aches within my chest.

Where is Korea
    On this giant blue swirl?
    Will I chance to find it
    If I spin and spin and jab?
    Will I crush him?

Is Korea red and orange now?
    Redorange-redorange-redorange
    Redorange-redorange-redorange
    Gun fire at sunrise
    Cannon fire at sunset

America is there to justify its cause
    One that its forgotten and left to crows
    Who tear it apart in partisan gulps.
    She took our boys
    She took our men
    Their souls have nowhere to go.

I cannot write my letters
    To the soul he keeps entombed.
    Instead I sit on the stained wood floor
    And write to the cold spot in his room.

* * *

My love is gone
    Perhaps to die
    As a cold spot
    In a room.

A poem by Jane Becker, published in the Meridian University Herald. Published 1951.

—

The Confession

Bless me, Father, for I have sinned
    And picked apart my souls for you
    If only heaven would take me in

It festers underneath my skin
    Their twisted humanity askew
    Bless me, Father, for I have sinned

Funny how my loves begin
    By planting wretched muck anew
    If only heaven would take me in

Wrinkled babies of string and tin
    Held together with hope and glue
    Bless me, Father, for I have sinned

I cut each out with Christmas gin
    And left them bawling, black and blue
    If only heaven would take me in

To kill off sadness, anger's twin,
    Confessing all is what I do
    Bless me, Father, for I have sinned
    If only heaven would take me in

After lunch, Junior helped Jane into her chair in the living room. The TV was dark. The room was quiet. He set the creme-colored on the small table along Jane's left side and the sheet of paper with Rose's number next to it.

"I can work from the house, so I'll be in the kitchen if you need anything. That way you can have privacy."

Jane nodded. She took a deep breath, then she picked up the phone and tapped in the numbers. She listened to the rings and caught herself counting them. It went to a voicemail.

Jane cleared her throat. "Hello, Rose. It's your mom. Give me a call when you have a chance. Some time today." Then she hung up.

Jane felt a lump in her throat dissolve. She felt a small relief. She set the paper aside and sighed. She picked up the remote and was about to hit the power button when the phone rang. The lump returned. Jane picked up the receiver.

"Hello?"

"Hi, mom."

Jane's stomach twisted to hear her eldest daughter's husky soprano. Rose had worn her voice away with smoking and drinking and screaming, but there was still music in it.

"It's been a while, mom."

Jane tried to clear her throat, but it refused her.

"How are you?"

"I'm... I'm good. Well, no. I'm concerned. I saw Lily's message, and I've been thinking about it. But before the message I was good."

Jane nodded.

"How are you?"

"Oh... just finishing some things up."

"Am I one of those things?"

"I suppose."

"I wondered if you'd call."

"Well, dear, the phone certainly works both ways."

The air chilled a bit.

"Cool. Awesome. What are we? Five minutes in?"

Jane sat in ice. She felt like hanging up the phone. She was very tired from her day, and there was still so much left.

"Rose-"

"I needed a mom."

"I was your mom," Jane retorted, a little hurt.

"No, you were my judge," Rose said. Her words were ice.

"Rose-"

"Every phone call, mom, had a ticking clock toward a lecture on the immorality of-"

"Rose, your lifestyle-"

"It's not a lifestyle, mom, it's my life."

"-not aligned with what God-"

"God?"

"Yes, with what God-"

"Where the hell was God when dad died, huh?"

Jane took controlled breaths in and out.

"I guess God was too busy judging me for the way he made me to save dad's life."

In and out. Chin shaking.

"Thanks for the talk, mom," Rose said. Her words were knives. "Always a pleasure."

"Rose," Jane said at last. "I love you."

"That's all you have to say? Not I'm sorry?"

Jane felt her eyes welling up. The living room was swimming in emotions.

"I'm not sorry for what I said, but I'm sorry for how it made you feel," Jane said.

Jane heard Rose's breath dancing. Jane heard a squeak on the other end. It sounded like a sob, but Jane realized it was a scoff.

"Thanks, mom. That means a lot," Rose said. Her words were poison. "Mom, I needed you. I miss you."

"I miss you, too, Rose."

Jane was crying. The tears dropped to the blanket draped across her knees and left dark discolorations on the fabric.

"I just wanted you to love me."

"Oh, sweetheart, I do love you. Why do you think I worked so hard to save you?"

"Save me? Huh. Yeah. That's fine. This isn't the big love fest that I thought it would be but whatever. It's not your style. I'll just have a good scream into my pillow tonight and be done with it."

Jane's eyes cleared a little. She could make out Junior's shape in the doorway. When her eyes met his, he looked away and went back into the kitchen.

"Rose..."

"Yeah, mom?" Rose sniffed.

"It's my fault you never got that bike."

"Um, what?"

"You wanted a bike for your tenth birthday. I convinced your father to get you a doll instead. I didn't think you'd actually use the bike. You… you were heartbroken for ages. You talked about it all the time. I'm really sorry."

"Thank you. That is a much better apology."

Jane sighed, deeply.

"I'm very tired, dear."

"I understand. You need your rest. I'm sure you have other things to finish up. Thank you for calling."

"Thank you for answering."

"I love you, mom."

"I love you, too, Rose."

"Good-bye."

Jane's mouth formed the words, but she said nothing. The handset slid down her chest and thudded into her lap. She tried to raise her arm to place it back on the side table.

"Junior?"

Junior came in from the kitchen. He replaced the receiver.

"How's Rose?"

"Better. I hope. I'm ready to nap."

Junior nodded. He fetched the blanket and some neck pillows. He propped and draped and arranged. When she was settled and comfortable, he kissed her on the cheek. He went to the kitchen to fetch his things, and, before he returned to the living room, Jane was fast asleep.

A letter from Rose Becker to Santa Claus. Dated December 10, 1960.
—

Dear Santa,

My name is Rose Becker. I am nine years old. I really wanted a bike for Christmas, and you gave me a doll instead. I don't like dolls, and I was really mad when you brought me one. My brother John told me to write you a letter so you'll give me a bike because you think I deserve it. I don't think I am very good at writing letters but I hope you like my letter.

I need a bike because I want a job giving people newspapers. My brother Jake gives people newspapers and he makes a lot of money. He can give out a lot of newspapers because he has a bike. He got a bike when he was ten and now he's twelve. I am only nine but I still think I should get a bike. With a bike I can give newspapers to everyone in the city and not even be tired and it would still be light out. I am fast at running so I think I would be fast at riding a bike, too.

I would take really good care of my bike. My dad has lots of rags in his shed. I would clean the bike every day before riding it. I would check the tires and make sure they are full of air. If a tire doesn't have enough air, I can ask dad to fill the tires up until they are full. If I got a nail in a tire, I can take the nail out and be careful so I don't get cut. My dad can help me fix the tire. If the handlebars come off the bike, I can ask my dad how to fix them. My dad is good at fixing things.

I can keep the bike in the shed where Jake and Junior have their bikes. There is enough space in the shed for three bikes or four bikes if you bring one for my little brother James. If you have to choose between me or James getting a bike, please choose me. James is not very careful with his toys. He breaks them a lot, and he doesn't take care of them. He leaves them out and the baby gets at them. I would never leave my bike out. I am very careful.

I want a bike because I love going fast and seeing all the things in the town even things that are far away. We live by a lake, and I can bike all around it and see all the animals and people and houses around the lake. I think that would be a lot of fun and help me be active. I like to learn new things. I love to spend time at the lake by myself and see interesting things. A bike would be a very good way to do that.

I hope this letter convinces you to bring me a bike even though it isn't Christmas any more. I am a good girl, and I am very careful with my things.

Thank you! Merry Christmas!
Rose Becker, age 9.

"Nurse Gladstone! A word?"

Nurse Gladstone quickly disappeared into nurse's station 2B when she heard Rose coming. Rose was practically running down the hallway. She was rounding the desk when a figure stepped into her path. Rose stopped short.

"Leann, out of my way," Rose fumed. She tried to step around her.

"Let's talk."

"Leann, I have an issue-"

"I told her not to do it, so your issue is with me."

"You-!"

Rose turned deep crimson. She pursed her lips and stormed away toward the locker room. Leann followed. She closed the door gently behind them. Rose was facing her locker, shaking with rage.

"If you ever-" Rose began.

"My job is to heal patients, so is yours. It's not to let ego-crazed doctors take their frustrations out on people."

Rose wheeled around.

"You didn't hear how he was talking to me."

"Yes, I did."

Rose laughed. "Did Nurse Gladstone tattle-"

"You think I wasn't going to follow you down that hallway and make sure you didn't hurt anyone? I know how you lash out when you're angry. So that's exactly what I did."

"I am a doctor."

"You're a wonderful doctor."

"No, stop it. I'm not fishing for compliments. I'm saying that I am a doctor. I put in my time and energy—everything—to become a doctor. A fantastic doctor. And that shriveled, senile old man has the nerve to-"

"What he said was inappropriate and demeaning."

"Thank you! So you see-"

"But what you almost did was illegal."

Rose pursed her lips again.

"Honey, let's sit down."

Leann took Rose's hand. Rose tried to resist. Leann laced her fingers between Rose's. Rose softened. They sat on one of the wooden benches that ran parallel to the lockers. They sat with their knees together, their hands together, their heads angled together. Rose sighed.

"You can't change him."

"I can punish him."

"Well, sure. But that won't change him. He'll still call you the same patronizing nicknames that he's used since he was a boy. He's an old man, set in his ways, and it's not worth his time to change or your time to try."

Rose scoffed.

"He's not worth your time. Just smile, bite your cheek and ignore it."

"That's always your answer! How can you say that? How can you just let things happen to you?"

Leann shrugged. "I have lots of practice."

Rose pulled her hands free and put her face in them.

"You're not really mad at him," Leann continued. "You're mad at her."

"Ugh. Well, he deserves my wrath as much as she does."

"No," Leann said, putting her hand on Rose's leg. "She deserves your forgiveness."

Rose lifted her head and looked Leann fully in the eyes. She shook her head sadly.

"You've lost your mind."

"No, I'm serious," Leann said. She was earnest and steadfast in her gaze. "Jane can't change. She's too old. There's a time in peoples' lives where they just can't change any more. It's like we're born as clay, but there's a timer on the stove. People just run out of time being clay and finally turn to pottery."

Rose rolled her eyes. "Oh, boy. I bet you're proud of that."

Leann punched Rose in the shoulder.

"I am! I just came up with it. I thought it was really clever."

Rose smiled. It cleared her clouds away. She put her head on Leann's shoulder.

"You're right. It was very clever."

Leann brought her hand up to Rose's cheek and held it.

"I'm not asking you to forgive Mr. Janes. He seems like an ass who has a lot to learn. Forget him. But you need to forgive your mom."

Rose checked her watch.

"It's late. Might be too late."

"Well, even if it is, it still isn't. You know?"

Rose sat up. "Do I call her?"

Leann shrugged. "It's a start. But first, you should apologize to Nurse Gladstone."

Rose hung her head. She ran a hand through her hair and nodded.

"Yeah, you're right."

"And you should remove that order before the interns start their shift. Mr. Janes looks like a colonoscopy would rip him apart."

A letter from Jane Becker to Rose. Undated.
—

Dear Rose:

When you read this, I'll be dead. As the hours wind down, I'm making a concerted effort to tie up loose ends and pass on the things that I think my children would appreciate the most. I've struggled most with what to impart to you. The best I can do with my physical possessions is say that you're welcome to have whatever isn't claimed so far.

Of interest to you, however, might be a small book of poetry. The poet listed on the front is Jane Keller. It may surprise you to know that I was a writer once. Not for long and not with much success, but I was published and paid. I wrote most of the poems in my high school and college days. This was before I had kids to raise.

There's a poem in there called "New America." I wrote it when your father was in the Korean War. It was a difficult time for me. I went through some real turmoil. I eventually left college and went back home to live with my parents until he came back. I really struggled with the reality of sending someone you love to kill people you've never met in a place that you don't really believe exists.

That's not the whole story, though. "New America" was a turning point for me and for those at college who were frustrated with the country's attitude about the war. It became, against my wishes, a rallying cry for those who were disenfranchised and angry. I was angry, sure, but I wasn't violent. I have never been violent.

People were hurt because of my words, and I never forgot that. It caused me to see how art can be a force that works against the artist's desires. Instead of change, I produced upheaval, violence and then return to status quo. I was expelled and never returned to school.

You might think that I treated you differently from the rest. I wanted to protect you from the world, Rose. You are special and different, and I know what the world has the power to do to people like that. I'm telling you about the poetry hoping that maybe you'll think more kindly on me knowing that I once fought for something and it beat me. It wasn't the only time the world beat me up. I always got back up, but I didn't always fight for myself. You've always been stronger than me in that sense.

I hope you'll read the poetry and forgive me for how I tried to protect you. Never stop fighting, Rose. That is a lesson that I learned way too late.

Love forever and always,
Your mother,
Jane Becker

Chapter 8

James casually flicked open his hip holster and pulled out his cellphone. He studied the screen down the end of his nose before answering the call.

"Hello, Lily."

"Hey, James. I've been calling all the siblings. Have you heard anything about mom today?"

"Mom? No, I haven't."

He heard Lily take a deep breath on the other end.

"Do… do you have time to talk?"

"Sure!" he chirped. "Sure, sure."

"Okay, well, I don't know if you can tell by my voice, but this is pretty serious."

"Serious? Why? Is something wrong with mom?"

"Well, I don't know. But I'm calling because there might be something wrong."

James was in a garage surrounded by real estate lawn signs. They were set neatly along the walls and stacked on shelves that lined the garage. A laptop where he'd been taking inventory glowed dimly on a work desk next to him. The tone in Lily's voice made the room sway a little. James looked around for a chair and found a wheeled stool tucked underneath the desk.

"I need to sit down."

"Let me know when you're ready," Lily said with the patient tone of a storied teacher.

James sighed. "Okay. I'm ready."

"Okay. This morning, everything was normal with mom's body, but she said she felt different. She told me that she's going to die today."

James thought about this.

"Why?"

"I don't know, James. There doesn't seem to be anything wrong, like, with her body. She doesn't seem sad. But she's doing a lot of things today. She's been to church, she went to coffee, she's been making phone calls. But she told me that she's going to die today. I thought you should know."

"Oh. Okay."

James felt numb. There was tingling in his cheeks.

"What should I do?"

"Well, James, what do you want to do?"

"I want to see mom. I should help her."

"Sure. That's a good idea. Can you leave work? You should talk to Junior before you leave."

"Yeah. Okay. I'll talk to Junior."

"Okay. You talk to Junior. I have to go back to work now, James. I'll talk to you later, okay?"

"Okay. Thanks, Lily."

"Bye. Bye, bye."

"Yup. Bye."

James ended the call and slid the phone back into its holster. He sat on the stool, quietly pivoting back and forth. His gaze was unfocused and serious. Behind him, the laptop went to sleep.

Jane awoke after ninety minutes of sleep. Nothing in particular roused her. The TV was still on in the living room. Another TV was on in the kitchen. The kitchen was playing sports highlights. Jane's TV was showing muted westerns.

"John?"

A chair scraped in the other room. The head that popped in wasn't what Jane was expecting.

"James?"

"Hi, mom."

James, a full head shorter than Junior and half a person wider, entered the room and walked to her chair. James still had his hair, and it still had most of its color, but he was otherwise the spitting image of his eldest brother. James smiled. His eyes sparkled and creased with well-worn laugh lines.

"Where's your father?"

"Dad?" James frowned. "You mean Junior, right? Junior and dad have the same first name."

Jane stared at him a moment. Then she blinked.

"Right. Junior. Where is he?"

"He had to get stuff from the store. I wanted to see you and to help you. He asked me to help you until he got back."

"Okay."

James knelt on the carpet next to the chair. "How are you doing?"

"Oh, fine, James."

James nodded. He clicked his tongue.

"Good. Good, good."

"How are you, James?"

James nodded his head a dozen times, looking around himself for the answer.

"Fine. Fine, fine."

"Good," said Jane. The nodding continued, but he said nothing more so she turned her attention to the TV. Jane had the vague feeling of knowing the show, but she had no precise memory of it. Jane glanced at her son. He had stopped nodding and was watching the show with great interest. Jane tried not to compare her children, but James stood out as a simple soul. He was pure but unfinished.

Jane cleared her throat. James's head whipped around. He began to stand.

"Need something, mom?"

Jane nodded and started to pull the blanket off. James grabbed the corner of it from her hand and yanked the blanket off in an exuberant flourish. The movement knocked her knees together, and she winced with the sharp pain. James didn't notice, and Jane was recovered quickly.

"Bring over my walker, please," Jane asked.

James fetched the walker from its corner and brought it over to her. He set it right in front of her chair.

"Turn it around," Jane said, and James rotated the walker so that the handles were facing her. She reached up and got handholds on the device.

"Don't let the chair spin," she told James. He placed a foot against the side of the chair as insurance. With both hands secure, Jane stood. Reaching her full height, Jane nodded at James.

"Thank you," she said.

James backed away to give Jane space. She inched toward the kitchen. James helped her into her chair, took her order and began making her lunch. As James heated her food, Jane stared out the large bay windows in the kitchen that overlooked the lake at the foot of their hill. The lake was shallow but usually teaming with fish. Jane had seen birds gathered by the hundreds, dotting the lake's surface. From her current vantage, however, Jane could only see the top of the grove of ash trees. James brought the food and a glass of to her.

"Silverware?" she asked.

"Oh! Right," James said and dug into the utensil drawer. "Right, right."

He produced a spoon, fork and knife and set them around her plate. Jane grabbed the fork and began to eat. James sat at the table right next to Jane. He watched her eat some, then he watched the show on the television, then he stood up. He clapped and rubbed his hands together as he wandered around the dining area. He looked over some of the family photos on the wall. He wandered to the large bay window. He stared intently at something.

"Mom, you should see this."

Jane looked up from her food. "What is it?"

"The birds! All over the lake! Can you see all the birds from there?"

Jane looked out the window again. All she could see was James and the sky around James.

"No."

"Well, you gotta see this. I've never seen so many birds in my whole, entire life."

James came around the table in a flash. He pulled her seat away from the table. Surprised, Jane dropped her fork, still wearing her next bite. James rotated her chair to face the lake.

"What about now?"

Jane saw the wall.

"No."

James thought for a moment. He went around to the front of the chair, reached under and drug the chair across the room toward the window.

"Now?"

Jane saw only the wall. It was larger.

"No," she said.

James squatted down behind her. "Oh! Now I see!"

Jane craned her head around to watch as James went to the far end of the dining table. He yanked hard, and it separated in the middle. The leaves pulled apart unwillingly. James flushed them against one side or the other, then he went around to the near side. He gave it a hard push. The leaves snapped back together. The table inched a little away from the window. He did this routine until he'd gained a whole foot.

James went back to Jane's chair. He slid her along the space he'd created. Jane was fully in front of the window now. She could see almost her entire front yard as it stretched down the hill and up to the road. Past the road was the shoreline.

"Can you see them now?"

"No."

"What? For real?" He pointed in a rough direction. "They're right- oh…"

There were birds on the lake, but only a few. They were in clumps of five or six and floating away from each other.

"Well, it was hundreds of them, all together on the lake. They weren't eating. Just sitting together. Maybe happy to have company. A duck meeting, but they can do the whole thing without talking. It was cool. I love birds."

Jane reached for James, but he was busy being busy. He pulled Jane back to her original position at the table. He rocked the table back into place. He straightened some of the placemats that had gone awry. James pushed Jane's chair in so she could finish eating. He put his hands on her shoulder, and she put her hands on top of his.

James stopped, and it lasted eternity. Then he bent down and hugged her. He wrapped his arms around her neck and touched his cheek to hers. He kissed her. She patted his arm with her hand. When he released her, Jane picked up her fork.

"Is it cold?" he asked.

Jane took the bite. She considered the morsel in her mouth and nodded. He took the plate to the microwave and reheated it. Jane looked at the TV but couldn't seem to watch it. A ding. The plate dropped in front of her, a little steam rising from its contents.

James gasped. "Mom! Look!"

James bent over to Jane's level and pointed out the side window she was facing. Hopping from feeder to feeder was a bright red cardinal. Jane gasped, too. She wondered if it was the same one from the restaurant. Jane laughed.

"See?" she said. "I did see the birds. You showed me the birds. And I love them."

James chuckled and hugged his mom again. They held each other like that as the cardinal made it each bird feeder. It pecked at the food and looked around. Moments later, it took to the air, and, in a crimson flash, it was gone.

A letter from Jane Becker to James. Undated.

—

Dear, James:

When you read this, I'll be dead. I know you are sad that I am dead, but I will see you again when you come to heaven. If you are sad or scared, you can always talk to Father at church. He can help you talk about your feelings.

You are very special to me, James. I will miss you very much when I am gone. I am happy that I will see you later. I want you to keep being a good worker for Junior. I know you will be a good worker. Remember to be a good listener.

I also want you to be a good helper for Lily. She might need your help when I am gone. She will need someone strong to help her move things around the house. She might give thing away from the house. Don't be mad at her, because it is her house now. Tell Lily what you want to keep. She will give it to you if she can, or she will help you find something else to keep.

Do you remember the cardinal we saw in the kitchen before I died? I think cardinals are very special birds. I hope that you think of me when you see cardinals. I will think of you when I see birds in heaven. Do you think there are birds in heaven? I hope so. I do love them.

I love you, James. I will see you soon.

Love forever and always,

Your mother,

Jane Becker

Chapter 9

Rebecca Nowack wiped tears away with her free hand. Her other hand held a shaky phone to her ear.

"I'll let you know if anything changes," Lily said.

"Yeah. Okay."

"Are you okay, Beck?"

"I just-"

"Mom?" Brandon asked as he came into the room. "Can you get me some cereal?"

"I have to go, Lily. Talk later." Rebecca hung up and admonished her son. "You can get your own cereal, Brandon. You know that."

Brandon groaned but slunk toward the cereal cabinet.

"But I wanted you to do it. I'm so worn out…"

He opened the door but before he could grab the cereal, Eli, younger by two years, swooped in. He ducked between his older brother and the cabinet and grabbed the box right under his nose.

"Hey!" Brandon shouted.

"Mom, can you get me a bowl?" Eli asked, sliding into his chair at the kitchen table.

"Try again," she said.

"Mom, can you please get me a bowl?"

"Thank you," Rebecca said, "and you boys know where the bowls are."

"Ugh!"

Rebecca left the kitchen and headed down the hall to the bedrooms.

She knocked on one door which swung open. Six-year-old Conrad was still on the bottom bunk, covers pulled up to the tuft of blond bed head.

"Time to wake up, sleepy head."

Rebecca sat on the bed. She rubbed Conrad's back.

"I'm sick, mom," said Conrad. He was facing the wall, so she had to lean over him to see his eyes. He looked up at her briefly, then his eyes darted back to the wall. Rebecca put a hand on his forehead.

"You feel okay. What's wrong?"

"My stomach hurts."

"You seemed fine last night. When did your stomach start hurting?"

"When I woke up."

Rebecca pulled the covers down to see him better. He wasn't in his pajamas any more. He was in his school uniform.

"You're already dressed?"

Conrad didn't acknowledge the question. Rebecca glanced at her watch and felt the minutes ticking away too quickly. She rubbed Conrad's back again and left the room.

"Can I stay home?" he called after her, but she didn't acknowledge the question.

Brandon and Eli had the TV on in the living room. Their spots at the table looked recently abandoned. Rebecca grabbed the remote out of Brandon's hand. She switched it off.

"Do we watch TV before school?"

"But they're talking about the game!"

"But you haven't cleared your spots. And have either of you brushed teeth?"

The boys exchanged a look. They groaned but got up and went to the kitchen. Rebecca went to the fridge and grabbed a white cheese stick. Brandon and Eli dropped their bowls into the sink.

"Don't forget to rinse," Rebecca reminded them, and she started back down the hallway toward Conrad. As she walked, she heard noise from behind one of the closed doors. She cracked it to see one-year-old Ann standing in her crib.

"Well, good morning, sweet pea."

Ann beamed and shrieked with a raw joy that only babies remember.

"I'll be right back," Rebecca told her and continued to the boys' room. Brandon and Eli ran passed her on their way to the bathroom, and Rebecca heard the start of their timer as she sat on Conrad's bed.

"Hungry? I brought you something."

She lowered the cheese stick into his eye line. He grabbed it and immediately peeled back the plastic.

"So…" Rebecca took a shot in the dark. "Anything cool happening at school today?"

"Yeah…" Conrad sounded despondent. "We have to spell in front of the whole class."

"Oh, really."

"Ten words, mom!"

"You have to spell ten words in front of everyone in your class?"

"Yeah!"

"That sounds kinda scary."

Conrad nodded, cheeks full of cheese. Ann called out from her room, joy tinged frustration. Rebecca had a little time.

"What sort of words do you have to spell?"

The timer went off in the bathroom. Rebecca heard a quick rush of running water and running feet. Her pocket buzzed from a text message.

"Wednesday."

Conrad pronounced the word like an evil spell.

"Oh, that's easy," Rebecca chirped. "W-I-N-D-Y. Wednesday."

"No, mom, that's windy. Spell Wednesday."

"Oh, right. W-H-E-N-S space D-A-Y."

Conrad giggled and turned over.

"No, that's not how you spell Wednesday."

"Oh, okay, okay. One more try: M-O-N-D-A-Y."

"No, that's Monday."

"Well, then you spell it, smarty-pants."

"W-E-D-N-E-S-D-A-Y!"

"Oh, my goodness! You're right! You're such a good speller."

Rebecca nudged him. Conrad grinned.

"I bet everyone will be so impressed with what a good speller you are." Conrad rolled his eyes, but he was still grinning. "And if you hurry now, you can have some applesauce before the bus gets here. But you have to run."

Conrad threw back the covers and ran out. Ann screeched when she saw him go by. Rebecca stood and fished the phone out of her pocket as she turned off the bedroom light and headed for Ann's room.

"Eat quick, Conrad," she called down the hall. "You still need to brush teeth."

Ann laughed and jumped in the crib to see her mom again. Rebecca smiled at Ann and glanced at the text message.

"can u bring lunch out? long day today. thx <3"

Rebecca put the phone away and picked Ann up. She held the little girl against her hip and carried her out.

"We'll change you later," she said.

Conrad snuck past them on his way to the bathroom. Brandon and Eli were watching a sports recap show on TV. Rebecca sat Ann on the couch between the boys and went to the fridge to start a bottle. Eli broke away from the TV and smiled at his little sister.

"Good morning! Good morning!" he cooed. "Are you ticklish?" He tickled her neck, and she started giggling. Brandon absent-mindedly leaned over and kissed Ann on the top of the head before returning his attention to the show. The timer went off in the bathroom, and Conrad came back sprinting into the living room just as the bus pulled into the view of their picture window.

Rebecca handed the bottle to Ann who immediately started sucking. Rebecca grabbed the remote again and turned off the show.

"Moooooom!"

"Bus is here. Grab your bags."

All three boys groaned.

"I love you! Have a great day!"

The boys went to the mud room and grabbed shoes, coats and bags. Rebecca opened the front door and kissed them each on the head as they filed out. She watched them all the way to the bus. She waved as it turned around and headed for town. She closed the door and stood for a moment, just staring.

Rebecca felt trapped in motion, although the house was still again. She had the vague memory of being interrupted in the midst of something. The bus passed out of sight, and Rebecca remembered the phone call she'd gotten just minutes ago. She began to cry.

A letter from Marshall Everett to Jane. Dated January 15, 1966.
—

Marshall Everett
Associate Editor
Midway Publishing, Inc.

Mrs. Becker:

My name is Marshall Everett, and I'm an Associate Editor with Midway Publishing, Inc. Part of my job is to go through the pile of manuscript submissions we get every quarter, called the slush pile. This week, your manuscript came across my desk, and I started this letter right away. I loved it!

The Barn is such an interesting look at life on a midwest farm at the early part of our century. Your characters have a real depth and magnetism to them. The journey they go on, physically and spiritually, is really quite something. I don't think I've read anything like it, and I read quite a bit.

The main character of Mary is such a strong and outspoken protagonist. I love how she won't let herself be ruled by the men in her life. She truly has her own agenda and desires. It's such a fresh take. I read so many female characters that do nothing of substance. This feels like a real woman. You obviously see her so clearly.

You might be wondering what happens next. Well, now that I've discovered the story, I'll pass it up the chain. It'll go to a Senior Editor, who will weigh in with his advice. He'll offer some edits or critiques, which you're free to ignore. Then it'll go to the Directory of Author Advocacy for the final nod and contract. That's also the time when the company might end the agreement if the book doesn't feel like a good fit for us. Each of these men will send off letters letting you know how The Barn is doing.

We don't advise our customers to make any assumptions about their manuscript at this point. A lot can happen in the next two stages, and we don't want authors to make rash decisions. I tell everyone to wait until the contract is signed before you start spending the money. If you have questions, you can write or telephone our main office and ask for me.

Hoping this finds you well, and I'm looking forward to working with you.
Marshall

The lake road snakes closely against the shoreline. As Junior and Jane headed north, the road climbed out of the lake valley only to flatten into prairie and settle down again. Copses of trees marked the transition from lake shore to great plains, and the road bobbed between the two hazards: fallen trees on the left and a plummet into the waters of Lake Meridian on the right.

They crested the hill and the road swung out, nearly perpendicular, into the countryside. From highway to gravel driveway, their trip was twelve minutes of farmland and grass. The driveway divided two cornfields. It was straight for a quarter of a mile, then it turned and ducked into some trees. At the end of the driveway was a beautiful house and a garage and a family of six.

Rebecca came out of the house and waved to them. She wore blue jeans and a thick, checkered shirt. Her hair was jet black and pulled into a pony tail. She had the lean build of a runner, but her face was lined with the long hours of being a farmer's wife. She smiled as she waited for them to pull up.

Junior stopped on the carpark. He helped Jane out, and Rebecca waited patiently nearby to greet them. When Jane was out and mobile, Rebecca swooped in for a hug and a kiss. She pulled back and rubbed her mom's shoulders. She couldn't stop blinking.

"Don't cry, Rebecca."

Rebecca closed her eyes to stop the tears, but they pushed out anyway.

"Are the kids around, Beck? Boys are at school, I suppose."

Rebecca wiped her eyes and coughed.

"Yeah. Ann is napping. The boys are still at school, so the house is pretty quiet."

She turned her attention back to Jane, putting a hand on her arm and speaking a little louder, she said, "Junior told us about supper. Are you excited about supper? The boys are really excited to have supper with you. Are you-"

"I thought the boys were at school." Junior muttered sarcastically. Rebecca narrowed her eyes at him.

"Well, they *will* be excited when they get home from school. Anyway, how do you feel? Do you feel okay?"

Rebecca was talking loudly, like Jane was on the other side of something expansive.

"Beck, she's the same mom you talked to on Sunday. She's not a child."

"I'm fine, Rebecca. Really," Jane said. She smiled at her daughter. Beck scrutinized Jane's face, searching for signs of duress or illness.

"But, mom, people who announce they're going to die are not usually fine."

"We've been over this."

"Well, I'm just saying-"

"She's not suicidal."

"How can you know what's going on in her mind? Maybe she's-"

"I've been with her most of the day and given her plenty of chances to kill herself. Trust me on this. She ordered me to leave a room filled with knives. Filled with them. Dozens of knives, all around her. No supervision."

Beck glared at her brother.

"Fine," she conceded. "Should we go inside?"

"She wants to see the barn."

"Of course. I'll be-"

"I want you to come with," Jane said. "Junior, can you watch Ann for her?"

"Sure. You two can spend some time together."

Beck was hesitant. "Are you sure, Junior?"

"Of course. Mom's probably getting sick of me, anyway. You guys go see the barn, and I'll have coffee or something in the house when you're done."

Jane and Beck nodded. Junior gave Jane a hug, punched Rebecca at the shoulder, and jogged over to the house before she could punch back. Jane turned her walker, and the women headed toward the barn.

A short story by Rebecca Becker. Dated March 7, 1969.
—

When the daddy woke up, he saw the stars. They were beautiful and surrounded him with their glow, crunchy and bright like new snow on a cold day. He reached out and plucked one. It was cold, like a diamond. The edges cut into his fingers, and the diamond dripped with his blood.

He pushed the diamond into the soil at his feet, and the ground bulged and swelled. A pregnant mound of mud grew and grew until it burst. Glowing, flaming mice swarmed out of the hole. They swarmed over the work boots of the daddy. He tried to stomp them and felt their small skeletons splintering. He stomped them into gunpowder.

The wind came up and tossed the gunpowder into the air. It circled around him and blotted out the stars and the diamonds. The surviving mice heard the deaths of their sisters and returned for revenge. The wind blew the gunpowder into their fur, and they exploded into popcorn. The daddy could smell smoke and butter. The daddy was hungry, and he scooped up some popcorn to eat but it was cold, hard porcelain.

He pushed the popcorn into the soil at his feet, and the ground danced and wiggled. Green stalks of corn jumped out of the dust and became as tall as skyscrapers. The wind played a song for them, and they danced like grownups, rooted and muted. Their giant, yellow ears blotted out the stars and the diamonds and left the daddy to muse on his views in the dark. He dug into the dirt and discovered the diamond he had planted. He held it up, and it glowed like a star and singed his skin. He let it go, but it hung in the air and gave him enough light for the rest of his days.

The daddy reached down and plucked the porcelain from the ground. It wasn't popcorn, it was a baby girl, pink and curled like a pig's tail. He cupped her in his hand, and she started to squirm and cry. He made a bed for her from the corn leaves so she was comfortable and cradled and cared for. The little girl was just opening her eyes when the star fell and touched the daddy on the head.

He fell and failed and forgot. The little girl cried and cursed and clawed. The star was alive, and it wrapped up the daddy like a present to keep for itself. Forever. And the little girl opened her eyes, but the daddy kept his closed. Forever.

The wind brought a chill and the scent of animals and smoke with it. It chilled Jane to her bones, and she shook in front of the giant, red structure. It was a barn, but not Jane's barn. It was Rebecca's barn, built with her husband, Ivan, and a contractor from town. It stood on the same spot as Jane's barn, but it was modern throughout. The reds and whites were as vibrant as if it'd been painted yesterday.

"You want to see the old barn, don't you."

Jane gave Rebecca a look of surprise.

"I'll show you what I mean."

They went around the barn to the back side. Beck hunched over and scanned the grass for something. She stayed close to the doors on the back side of the barn. One hand trailed along the siding as she walked. Then she stopped. She flagged Jane over. "Here it is!"

Jane shuffled to Rebecca's spot. Rebecca was pointing down, moving some of the dirt with her foot. Jane bent to see. In the ground at Rebecca's feet was a small square of cement with the letter "K" etched into it.

"We found that during demolition. We're pretty sure it was a foundation stone of some sort. Maybe the corner stone. Do you know?"

Jane did know. And she was transported to this very farm, at this very spot, where her father was showing her the very same stone.

"It marks our barn," he'd said.

"But our barn will mark our barn," Jane had said, confused.

"Not if it burns down. This helps us know where to rebuild."

The farm was bustling with life. Jane's brothers and father were measuring and cutting and constructing like they were in a race. They needed a new barn. The loan had been substantial, something Jane's mom fretted about constantly. There were others there, too. People Jane didn't know who rushed around and helped the men do everything.

"I hope we never have to rebuild. I hope we'll be happy here forever."

Jane threw her arms around her dad's leg. He rubbed her back and mussed up her hair.

"Oh, you'll leave some day," Jacob said. "But you'll come back. And this will mark your spot."

The barn had been a monument to the possibility of their land. The land held enormous potential in Jacob's eyes. He need only dare to realize it.

Mary Jane had smashed a bottle of wine against the side of it and chipped a fleck of bright red paint off. Everyone ate and drank under tents in the front yard, in full view of it. The flavors had been unlike any Jane had ever had, and her head swam with the scents and tastes of everything. Jane had never seen her father smile so brightly as that night.

Under a gigantic moon, she chased her brothers and friends around and through and back into the moonlight. The air was still warm with summer, but a cool breeze surprised them now and then. Running made her feel infinite. She passed by her father, and he grabbed her round the middle and tossed her into the air. Jane hung there next to the moon, untouched by gravity for a moment. But she had come back down the earth, caught in Jacob's arms and settled gently on the ground.

"Mom? Do you remember the corner stone from when you were a kid?"

Jane blinked and came back. She saw so many years etched onto it.

"I remember."

"Do you want it? I can have Ivan dig it up for you."

"No, dear. It marks the barn."

Rebecca nodded and rubbed Jane's shoulders as they shivered in the wind.

"Do you want to see inside the barn?"

Jane shook her head.

"If you've seen one barn, you've seen them all."

A letter from Nic Schwartz to Jane. Dated March 28, 1966.
—

Nicolas Schwartz
Senior Editor, Literary Fiction
Midway Publishing, Inc.

Mrs. Becker:

In light of recent disagreements by post and telephone, I hope it is no surprise that you find this letter without a contract packet. I can appreciate an artist's desire to maintain her vision of integrity, but I feel we've reached a creative impasse on this project. The views of the author and the views of the publisher are too at odds. A few examples come to mind.

A major aspect of the novel that I felt needed work was Mary as an adult. I see in her too much of the younger Mary. We all grow out of our youthful ways into reasonable adults. Mary does not follow that course in her life. She continues to push back on traditions, and it's obvious it creates a lot of stress on her family. I applaud how you explored that approach for your character, but I don't think readers will enjoy being that uncomfortable for that long. Readers want a woman to bring harmony to the home, and they want womanly characters to bring harmony to the story.

Previously, I marked a chapter for "Strike" that you seemed to have missed in the edits. It is now my belief that you didn't miss the sheet and instead decided to ignore the critique. Rather than discuss this with me, you maintained the chapter even into the final round of edits.

The chapter seems innocuous enough to some. In it, young Mary learns to drive an automobile. To our readership, it is unimaginable. An informal survey found that most readers were made deeply uncomfortable by the chapter. They had concerns that Mary was too nervous during the lesson. They became convinced she would have a wreck and get injured during the scene, which she thankfully didn't. Worse still, the chapter reminded them of how quickly hysterics can reduce a female driver to a roadside casualty. If you imagine you can sell this book with that chapter intact, you have much to learn about the art of selling books.

The other problematic chapter is the bread pudding scene. We have performed our own tug of war over the tone of that scene, and it seems we cannot reach a compromise. I noticed your latest version is the original version. I was even able to check it against our archive, and you maintained it verbatim. I truly felt we had made some progress on that front. Creative interpretations are one thing, but flagrant disregard for the level-headed and sound recommendations of a professional editor is another thing entirely.

Our difficulties with this book illustrate clearly to Midway Publishing, Inc., that we are not a good fit for your book. We will not be drafting a contract with you or pursuing further edits on the manuscript. We wish you best of luck with your story.

Sincerely,
Nicolas Schwartz

Ann was awake when they got back to the house. Junior was kneeling on the floor watching a football game and absentmindedly shaking a toy where he thought the baby was. Jane maneuvered to the couch. Rebecca discovered where Junior had started to make coffee before getting distracted. She started the brew and warmed a bottle for Ann at the same time.

Jane caught Ann's attention with a big smile. Ann gave up on her lackluster uncle and crawled over. Ann brought a small ball with her as she crawled to Jane's spot. Ann climbed the couch to her feet and tossed the ball at Jane. She waited for Jane to fish it out from between the couch cushions. Jane handed the ball back. Ann threw it again and laughed.

When it was ready, Rebecca came into the living room with cups of coffee. She handed a steaming mug to Jane. She held one out for Junior who didn't notice. She had to tap him on the shoulder, and his sudden spasm nearly knocked it out of her hand.

"Who plays basketball in the middle of a weekday?"

"No one. It's from last night," Junior said. "But I missed it."

Rebecca sat next to Jane and held the bottle out for Ann. Ann threw the ball one more time and came climbing. Rebecca picked up the child, cradled her in the crook of her left arm, and handed her the bottle. Rebecca swayed and watched the baby. Jane reached over and touched Ann's foot. She gave it a playful shake. Rebecca smiled.

"You like babies, don't you, mom."

Jane smiled. "Why do you think I had so many?"

"Six is a lot."

"Oh, I had more than that."

Rebecca was surprised.

"What do you mean?"

"I had two babies before Junior. Stillborn."

"Oh, that's right. Eight babies."

"Eight darlings."

Rebecca shook her head.

"I have my hands full enough with four. I can't imagine how you did it."

"Once you have two, you know how to handle twenty. Just more bottoms to wipe."

They laughed together.

"Did dad like babies as much as you did?"

"Oh," said Jane, searching the air for an answer, "I think so. I mean, he never complained about having too many kids. He was always game for having more. We may have had more. You never know."

"Really?" Rebecca's sudden shock startled the baby, and the bottle popped out of her mouth. Ann grabbed it and quickly replaced it. "More than six? That's amazing. You're amazing, mom."

"Well, I was in my forties, so maybe not."

"Yes!" Junior shouted. He pumped his fist, careful to keep his coffee level. The ladies all gave him a moment's notice. Ann's eyes were getting heavy.

"I think about that sometimes."

"About having more kids?"

"No... About raising them alone. Farming's dangerous, especially at harvest. The hours are very long. Ivan doesn't get much sleep. The equipment is heavy and terrifying. We've all heard the horror stories. Lost limbs. Lost lives. How did you raise us after dad died?"

Jane smiled at Rebecca. "We raised each other."

"But it must have been hard. And chaotic."

"It was. Sometimes. But you kids all knew that we were in it together. I tried my best to be fair and patient and to be your leader. You were good, smart kids. Our lives weren't perfect. Everyone has some scars, but we got through it as a family. I think your father had a lot to do with that."

"How do you mean?"

The bottle was drained. Rebecca sat Ann up and rubbed and patted her back. Jane reached over for the bottle and set it on a table nearby.

"He worked hard, especially when you were young, to make everyone think like a family. Family votes. Let's vote as a family. Making the older siblings take ownership of the younger ones. Everyone was conditioned to work as a group and to look out for one another. That didn't go away when he did."

"You were a big part of that, too."

"Sure. He conditioned me, too."

Rebecca set Ann on the floor to crawl and play. She found Uncle Junior and started to climb his back. Rebecca watched them.

"Is that why you always had us doing puzzles? To build teamwork and bonding and collaborative problem solving?"

"No, that was so I could have a minute to myself for once."

Rebecca smiled. "Well, it worked. Puzzles and books."

"And cookbooks. I think I caught you reading those more than westerns."

"Oh, I love reading cookbooks. You know, as I've gotten older, I've realized that no one else does that. I'm the only person I've ever met who would read cookbooks like regular books."

"I know," said Jane, smirking.

"Well, I didn't! I guess I'm weird. I just get such a kick out of seeing all these little ingredients get mixed together into something entirely different and delicious. I barely look at recipes these days. I think I taught myself how to taste and identify enough ingredients, and I've practiced enough that I don't usually need it. But, man… hours and hours of reading cookbooks. Do you still have those books?"

"I should. In the office."

A surreptitious smile came across Rebecca's face. "Do you still have the secret cookbooks?"

Jane cocked her head. "What secret cookbooks?"

Rebecca pointed at her mom. "You remember! There was a whole shelf of cookbooks that you had way up high on a shelf in the office. Every time I asked if I could read them, you said no. The Manglemore Cook Book was one of them."

"The Mangalore Ladies Club Cookery Book."

"Yeah. What is that?"

Jane smiled in memory. "Well, it's a cookbook published by a charitable organization in India called The Mangalore Ladies Club. The club members share their recipes."

"India? Have you been to India?"

"Oh, no, but I ran with a pretty diverse crowd in college, and a friend of mine gave it to me as a gift. Her name was Shammi Kumar. There is a recipe in there for Meat Kofta Curry that is phenomenal."

"Kofta curry… I'll have to try that some day."

"Well, I can give you the recipe."

"Thanks, mom. But what about the Betty Crocker Cookbook you had up there? You let me read the one on the bottom shelf but not the one on the top shelf. Why did you have two?"

"Because the one on the top shelf was an original printing valued at almost a thousand dollars."

"What??"

Rebecca's eyes were huge.

"I let you read the fifteen dollar one instead."

"Yeah, no kidding. That's why I keep my original printing of The Joy of Cooking locked out of sight." Rebecca pointed at a small cupboard above the fridge. "Guess I know where I got that from."

Jane shrugged. "Didn't do me any good. I didn't think about it most of the time, and I rarely appreciated it. There's a lot in life I didn't appreciate enough."

Rebecca put her hand on Jane's. Ann climbed over, and Rebecca put her hand on top. The three of them sat like that until Ann got bored and crawled away again.

A letter from Jane Becker to Rebecca. Undated.
—

Dear Rebecca:

When you read this, I'll be dead. As the hours wind down, I'm making a concerted effort to tie up loose ends and pass on the things that I think my children would appreciate the most. I leave you two things. The first are my cookbooks. Yes, even the Betty Crocker. You alone appreciate them as much as I did, and you alone can give those recipes the care they deserve. I know you'll make some brilliant meat kafta curry.

It will probably surprise you and my other children that I'm a writer, although you won't see my name on any bookshelves or on any bestseller lists. You will, however, find a full length manuscript written by me and marred by vultures.

When you children were young, I decided to write a novel inspired by my childhood. It's called The Barn, and I found some interest in it through a Meridian publisher. The relationship was contentious and difficult, and after making many ugly compromises, the publisher decided not to draft a contract. At the time, I was devastated. Today, I am grateful.

I know you think of yourself as just a prairie wife. I know your focus is on your family. I also know that you used to write such beautiful little stories. You used to show them to me all the time, and I thought often of showing you The Barn, to encourage you as much as ask for your help on it. Well, I have a favor to ask of you. I would like you to use your creative and common senses to find a suitable publisher for The Barn. I think there's value in it. Maybe you and maybe now is the perfect combination.

This letter comes with a package. In the package is the revision of the novel that I sent to Midway Publications. They accepted it for revisions but rejected it when I refused to compromise my vision. The novel is the portrait of a strong, midwestern farm woman. Her whole life, from childhood to adulthood, centers around the family's barn, which is the lifeblood and cultural center for the family. It is threatened, used, burned down, rebuilt, ignored, modified and finally passed on to the next generation. The main character, Mary, loves the barn and despises it, and she has to make peace with each of those emotions.

My vision for the novel is that it maintain this tenet: a woman is like a barn. She is strong and vibrant. She is necessary and useful. She welcomes life into herself and makes life on the farm possible. She keeps things, like the history and stories of the family. And she can be destroyed and made into something less than she was. Please keep these ideas at the heart of the novel. Make it your own. Put your name on it. I don't need the fame. I just want the story to get told.

Another note: there is a scene with bread pudding. This scene is to stay as-is.

Love forever and always,

Your mother,

Jane Becker

Chapter 10

Lily sat at the kitchen table staring out at the lake. The wind was up, and the slate-gray water was capped in white peaks. The windows shivered and rattled. It was just before lunch, but it was dark. The clouds were heavy with thoughts of snow.

There were no birds on the lake or in the yard. The stalwarts who hadn't migrated couldn't handle the weather and were holed up in their nests. Just like Lily was holed up, safe from the weather, sheltered from the chill, tucked away from questions and stares.

She startled at a rapping at the front door. She stood and realized through stiffness that she must have been sitting there for a very long time.

"Coming," she called out to the visitor. She opened the door. Junior pushed through the storm door and the front door into the entryway. He had a box in his hands.

"Hey, little sis. How's it going?"

"What's that?" Lily asked, pointing to the box.

"Let's go see."

Junior handed the box into Lily's eager hands, and she took it into the kitchen. She heard the sounds of Junior kicking off his shoes, undoing his coat and shuffling in. He walked past the box toward the fridge.

"Everything where it used to be?"

"Yeah. It's too soon to rearrange anything."

Junior went to a cupboard and opened it up. He grabbed two small plates. Then he opened a drawer and pulled out two forks. He set everything on the table, arranged into two settings. Lily opened the box. The thin cardboard lid opened easily, and it swung all the way open. Inside was a bread pudding . There was a spatula already waiting for them. Junior grabbed the spatula and carved a liberal piece for Lily. He served himself, sat and readied his fork.

"Mom's recipe?"

"No, unfortunately. I went through that office three times looking for it, but I never found it. I got this off the internet and adjusted it."

"Tasted it?"

"Not yet…"

Junior and Lily plunged their forks into the golden-brown mounds of sweet bread. Lily took her bite. The bread was soft and moist with a hint of crust. The custard was sweet but with a slightly smokey flavor. It was rich and decadent and delicious.

"Not like mom's."

Junior nodded his head in agreement.

"No, but I like it."

Lily nodded. "I do, too. What's in it?"

Junior raised his eyebrow. "Secret family recipe."

"What?! Just tell me."

"No. If mom and Rebecca get to keep a secret bread pudding recipe, so do I. It's only fair. I'm the oldest."

"Well, I'm the youngest. I should get whatever I want."

"You did. You got this house."

"*And* I want the recipe."

Junior shook his head and went back to eating.

"Fine. I'll just make my own. We'll be The Family With 1,000 Bread Pudding Recipes."

"There's worse ways to get famous," Junior mused. "You know what this needs? Coffee. Do you want some coffee?"

"Sure," Lily said. "Know where the stuff is?"

Junior stood and went back to the cupboards.

"Same place mom always kept it?"

"Yup…"

Lily looked off into space.

Junior busied himself making the beverage. Lily decided to stop eating until she could pair it with the drink. She turned back to the lake. The waves were still arguing with winter.

"She would expect you to change things, you know."

Lily drew a long breath through her nose. She looked at Junior. He was pouring water into the coffee maker.

"I know. She was telling me I could change things the day I moved in. She didn't care. She's not as sentimental as the rest of us."

"Oh, I think she's plenty sentimental. She's just been knocked down enough to know that sentimentality is as useful as a paper hat in a rainstorm."

Junior scooped coffee into the filter, closed the top and hit the button. The machine started to bubble and percolate.

"Knocked down? You mean, because of dad?"

"I think there's more to it than just dad, but yeah. I've been trying to piece her life together. There's that whole box to go through yet. But imagine it: having to watch your husband die and then raise his six kids alone. I bet it changed her. I remember a little of it. She didn't get cynical, but she had a different perspective on things. I don't know. It was strange. She would get these bursts of energy, but then she'd always lapse back to being pragmatic. I wish I would have paid more attention. Now that she's gone…"

"You don't have a chance to ask her?"

Junior crossed the room and returned to his seat.

"Yeah." he said. "Would you?"

"Ask her?"

"Yeah."

Lily thought about it. "No? I mean, we had our chance. She gave us a heads' up. I suppose if there was anything I desperately needed to ask, it would have come to me already. 'What's your favorite band?'"

Junior laughed.

"What's your favorite color?"

"If you were stranded on a desert island with three books, what would they be?"

"And don't worry about food or drink. We've arranged for all that, so all you need to worry about is your book choice."

Lily chuckled. "Right."

"Actually, I do wonder what she would choose."

Lily stood up. "Let's figure it out."

"What do you mean?"

"That's still brewing. Let's go through her shelves and see what books are easy to reach, bookmarked, dogeared. You know? We can figure this out, and it'll give us something to do."

"I don't need anything to do."

"Fine, it'll give me something to do."

Junior shrugged.

"Fine," he said, "but the second that coffee is ready, I am nose-diving back into this bread pudding."

Jack Becker's obituary. Dated August 26, 1953.

—

Jackson Leo Becker, 34, died on August 22nd, 1953, in Meridian, South Dakota.

Becker was born on April 20th, 1919, in Meridian to Leo and Delores (Roebuck) Becker. He grew up in Meridian, graduating from Meridian East High School. He attended Guthrie College in northern Meridian and received a bachelor's degree in education. He attended General Beadle State College in Madison, South Dakota, and graduated with a master's degree in education. He returned to Meridian to teach at Meridian East High School until his death.

Jack married Ethel Keller on June 20th, 1945, at St. Thomas Aquinas Church in Stone City, South Dakota.

Survivors include his wife, Ethel; his parents; and his brother, Johnathon Becker, Sr.

The family has released the following statement about Becker's passing:

Jack was a deeply loved man. He had a great passion for people, especially his students, and for life. For some time, Jack has wrestled with demons. He found it difficult to open up about these struggles and often found himself in places of pain and darkness. We hope the community remembers Jack as a dedicated educator and a great lover of the things that make life special. Thank you.

The living room had many bookcases: next to her chair, next to the fireplace by the puzzles, two lining the lake-facing wall. Junior took the floor-to-ceiling bookcase, and Lily took the stouter one. Lily tilted her head sideways and squinted at the book spines. They were nearly pristine. Lily quickly made her way across the top shelf and dropped to the next one. The book looked untouched.

"These are in perfect condition," Junior said. "Did she even read most of these?"

"I think she read them all once. Most of them probably only once."

Lily finished her bookcase and moved to the one by the puzzles. One shelf was lined with portraits of the family. The other shelves had books, mostly western novels. Lily found the same thing: books barely read.

"If we ever sell these, they could probably go for a decent price," said Junior. "Well, as decent as used paperbacks get these days."

The bottom shelf held reference books. Their spines were cracked and worn. Lily remembered pouring through the encyclopedias, dictionaries and thesauruses for school assignments. Lily pulled a volume. As she was thumbing through "Sa-Sm", Junior finished his bookcase and made for the one by Jane's chair. Lily saw nothing noteworthy. She replaced the book and passed on the rest of the shelf. Lily put her hands on her hips and looked around the room looking for other caches of books.

"Mom has books in her room, right?"

"You tell me, person who lives here."

Lily stood in the doorway of Jane's bedroom in the darkness. A gray slant of light gave the furniture modest existence, and Lily could see the queen-sized bed, the trunk at the foot of it and end tables on either side. The tables were short, wooden things wearing lamps and boasting drawers. One of the tables had a telephone from the eighties still wired up.

Lily went to the left table, where Jane used to sleep. Lily had always wondered why she didn't just sleep in the middle, but she never asked about that. Lily sat on the bed. The mattress was stiff. It felt new. Maybe Lily would adopt it for herself. The bedclothes were in good condition but dated. Maybe Beck would want them. The alarm clock was ancient, and Lily had no feelings for it: rummage sale. Lily looked around the room. The blankets in the chest at the foot of the bed could be divided between siblings. Lily had plenty of blankets. The chest would stay. The lamps would stay. The side tables would stay. Lily felt a little lighter.

Lily opened the top drawer. Inside were pencils, playing cards, stacks of tiny notepads and prayer books. She scooped out about half of the contents and laid them on the bed. She started to organize them. The notebooks reflected all the eras of Jane's life: the real estate agency, the church, some just piles of scrap paper cut stapled. Lily made a mental note to flip through them later. The pencils, likewise, came from all over: small businesses, politicians, golf courses. They were of various lengths and sharpnesses and each had been used. Each pencil had been given some purpose for some duration and then given respite. Some had bite marks. Lily couldn't decided if they were worth keeping.

Lily set the pencils aside and looked at the books. Most of them had thin, black leather covers. Some had gold leaf brushed onto the thin side of the paper. The smaller books were no bigger than Lily's palm. The largest one was slightly larger than Lily's hand with her fingers splayed. Across the front, in sparkling gold leaf, it said "BIBLE."

Lily opened it. The inner cover was covered in gold, just like the side. There was a sheet of white tissue paper and then the cardboard-stiff dedication page. In a slanted and flat cursive was written, "To: My Blue J. From: John. My dearest, deepest love." Lily stared at her dad's handwriting for a long time. She traced the curve of the letters with her fingertips, and her heart fluttered.

A prayer card slid out from behind it. The card was thin and glossy with a heroic image of St. Michael the Archangel placing his foot on the hairy, goat-head of Satan. Lily flipped it over. There was the prayer to St. Michael. Lily turned the page, replaced the card and thumbed off a couple dozen more pages to flip to.

She found a folded sheet of paper. She unfolded it and gasped. It was the face of her father. Lily felt her heart racing away. She was holding the one-sheet from his funeral. The document was unfinished. The obituary was written in Jane's hand, and little red edit marks scored the paragraphs. Lily folded it neatly and replaced it and flipped again.

She stopped at another piece of paper. Lily unfolded this one more carefully but was again startled by what she found. It was a letter addressed to her. The light was too dim, so Lily reached over and illuminated the lamp. She poured over it, feeling wave after wave of emotion crash over her. Lily tried to absorb the letter. It was a commendation. It was an apology. It was permission. And, in all those things, it was perfect. The crashing stopped and relief washed over Lily. Peace slowed her shivering heart. Lily folded the letter and put it back.

There was a light knock on the doorframe. Lily looked up, tears clouding her vision. Junior framed the edge of the gray-lit room, a halo of white poured in from the lake-facing windows.

"What'd you find?"

"I found her favorite book."

John Becker, Sr.'s obituary. Dated November 16, 1968.

—

Johnathon Neil Becker, Sr., 48, died on November 12th, 1968, at his home in Stone City, South Dakota.

Becker was born on April 30th, 1920, in Meridian, South Dakota, to Leo and Delores (Roebuck) Becker. He grew up in Meridian, graduating from Meridian East High School. He attended Meridian University and received a degree in business administration. He returned home and started a successful real estate business, Becker Realty.

John married Jane Keller on September 23rd, 1948, at St. Thomas Aquinas Church in Stone City, South Dakota.

When John started Becker Realty, he was the sole realtor. The company grew and quickly became one of the best-known names in the real estate business in Meridian, Stone City and neighboring townships.

Survivors include his wife, Jane; his children: Johnathon, Jr., Jacob, Roselyn, James, Rebecca and Lillian.

He was preceded in death by his parents and brother, Jack.

The coffee was hot and ready when they got back to the table. The bread puddings had gone a little cool, so Junior popped them in the microwave. When they finished, pale trails of steam rose from their crusted peaks. He set the plates on the table and went back to the coffee maker.

"How do you want your coffee?" Junior asked, pulling two mugs out. Lily normally took her coffee with some cream and sugar, but she felt like something different today, something stronger. Something more like Jane.

"Black."

"Whoa. Full diesel."

Junior poured the drinks and carried them over to the table. He took his seat.

"Who's this new girl that takes her coffee black? Are you going to start drinking whiskey, too?"

"Yup. Straight from the bottle."

"So, you're jumping just straight into alcoholism then."

Junior and Lily dug in, washing down the delicious desert with hot, black coffee. When they were done, they both pushed back in their chairs and stared into space. Lily thought about her letter. She had never considered caring for her mother as work, but it truly had been a second job. They were both retired, and Lily was facing a large number of free hours.

What could her life be like now? She wouldn't hesitate when asked to go out on the town. She wouldn't need to make arrangements if she wanted to travel. She could watch something other than westerns. There were all sorts of opportunities afforded her now.

"What do I do now?" Lily asked the old house. "With my life?"

Junior exhaled loudly.

"Well, what do you want to do?"

"How is that a helpful response?"

"No, really. What is something from the back of your mind that you've always wanted to do but stopped yourself from even thinking?"

"Going to a movie?"

"No, bigger."

"With what my social life has been like, that's plenty big."

"And plenty easy. That'll happen. You don't have to plan that. You could do that today. Think bigger."

"Uh... I don't know. I'll have more time to read."

Junior rolled his eyes.

"Do you not understand what the word 'bigger' means? I thought you were an educator."

Lily lightly punched him on the arm.

"I love reading, and I never get enough time for it."

Junior rubbed his eyes with the palms of his hands. He ran his hands through his hair and then tented them over the bridge of his nose. He squinted in thought.

"Then go do it!"

"Well, you're here. I don't wan to be rude."

"Okay, fill in the blank. 'Now that I'm on my own, I can finally…'"

"Read more."

Junior grunted.

"Okay, sure. We covered that. Now that I'm on my own, I can finally…"

"Go out whenever I want."

"Come on, Lily. I can finally…"

"Travel… somewhere?"

Junior slammed his hand on the table.

"Bigger, Lily! Think! I can finally…"

"Go to Ireland!"

Junior slammed his hand on the table again.

"Perfect! When are you going?"

"What??"

"When are you going, Lily? Make a plan. Make a promise to yourself, right now."

"Junior, I just came up with this."

"I'm going to Ireland next…"

"I don't know."

Junior slammed the table again.

"Lily! I will smash this table in half with my anger. I'm going to Ireland next…"

"Someday?"

"That's not even a grammatical sentence. I'm really concerned for your students, you know? I'm going to Ireland next…"

"Summer. June!"

"Say the whole thing!"

"Now that I'm own my own, I can finally go to Ireland next summer in June!"

Lily felt adrenaline coursing through her body. Junior put up his hand for a high-five. The crack of their celebration hurt her ears. Lily tried to shake the pain out of her hand. Junior did his best to look unfazed, but she saw him cradle his own hand gingerly.

"Awesome! That's called a breakthrough. I should be a life coach."

"Well, this isn't exactly great life advice?"

Junior scoffed.

"What? This is perfect life advice. I'm getting you out of here and on the trip of a lifetime."

"Which I can't afford. And aren't you supposed to avoid making major life decisions after the death of a loved one?"

"Well… I mean, I'm not a financial coach or a grief counselor. You'll have to find other people for that."

Junior stood and collected the plates and silverware. He brought them to the sink and rinsed them. He returned to finish that last of his coffee. He reached for Lily's cup, but she waved him off clearing it.

"Keep the pot on," she told him. "I'll need to stay energized for this insane trip you convinced me to take."

Junior shrugged. "Or don't. The important part, and this is where my life coachery is really top notch: the important part is visualizing it. If you can visualize it, it's practically reality. The rest is just details. I read that somewhere important, like a newspaper."

Junior closed the lid on his bread pudding. He went to the fridge to find space for it.

"You can keep this. It's a parting gift for your big trip."

"I'm not leaving until June."

"Is that what we decided? I wasn't really listening. Another life coach tip: don't get invested in your clients. They are bad at life."

Lily stood and gave her big brother a hug, then she walked him to the door. She waited for him to get his shoes and coat back on. He kissed her on the cheek and tucked back into the wind and cold. As he left, she gave him a little wave.

Back in the kitchen, Lily's mug was still steaming. She caught a view of the lake, and watched it from her chair again. She lifted the coffee to her lips and let the beverage warm her. The lake was boiling with uncertainty and tumult. Lily watched the chaos pound into the granite shoreline time after time after time. And yet the shore stood fast and strong, eager to take on each new wave. The waves etch the shore just as the shore constrains the waves.

Lily sipped her coffee and wondered what color Irish waves are in summer.

A letter from Jane Becker to Lily. Undated.
—

Dear Lillian:

When you read this, I'll be dead. It may surprise you to find a letter written to you that you had no knowledge of. Your mother works in mysterious ways. Yours is the first of hopefully many letters. There's so much I need to say and so much I want to say but also so much I've never been allowed to say.

I think my passing will be hardest on you. You and I have been a team for decades but most especially after your husband passed on and my health began to fail. Your father saw you as a blessing for me in my twilight years. He wanted to give me a child to see me through to my end. You were his last present to me, but you've been so much more.

You are someone who has become dependable, thoughtful, gracious and selfless. This last year in particular has been hard on me, physically. You've always been at my side, ready and willing and able to throw yourself into my service. You get up with me when I need help. You stay up with me when I need company. You help me cook and clean. You help me bathe and dress. You are such an important part of my life, and I cherish every moment.

I hope you don't resent me or your father. You were made for this purpose and saddled with these responsibilities before even your conception. I'd always wondered how you'd bear the weight of this life, and whether you'd truly be there for me when I needed you. People do not always embrace their destinies. You were always steadfast, calm and willing, and you have no idea how much that meant to me.

When I think back on it, I know exactly what it must have meant for you. It meant stopping your life to continue mine. You never complained, at least not to me, but I know it must have affected your life. I helped take care of my own mother in her final days. It's a thankless job, and it means waiting. Waiting for an end. Waiting to be yourself. Good news: I'm finally gone.

All this is to say thank you.

I'm leaving this letter in my bible. This bible is my favorite book. I got it as a wedding gift from your father, and he wrote a message to me on the inside. I've used it to couch the prayer cards from every baptism, confirmation, wedding and funeral. It seems like hoarding, but each one is significant in some way. They each represent a part of me. You'll find quite a few of your own milestones in here.

This bible also has my notes in it. Over the years, I've come to use the book as a living document open to interpretation and reinterpretation. My notes are a sort of layman's commentary on the events and teachings in the bible. The comments may be useful. They may be interesting. They may be heresy. It's too late for me to do anything about it now.

If you're wondering what to do with my bible. Let me make the case for your keeping it. It's a rather eloquent and simple translation. It was written simply for those preparing for their first communion. The language is plain and straightforward, casting off all highfalutin vocabulary. It reads the way people speak, and I've always found that to be a great comfort.

You will find surprises in these pages, too. You, personally, Lillian. I've had the opportunity to learn and remember some of your favorite passages, and I've jotted notes next to them. I've made my own observations and reflections when praying on those same verses. Perhaps you'll find some sort of kinship or solace in that.

I know you well enough to feel certain in that whatever you decide will be the right choice.

Love forever and always,

Your mother,

Jane Becker

Chapter 11

If it burns down, we know where to rebuild. Then he smiled at me.

I am in mama's arms. She holds me so tight my legs are pinned against her ribs and under her arms. It's painful. Some thick sickness in my stomach keeps bobbing up. Her hand pushes on my back. It's painful. Orange and red on black. In blobs. In streaks. It's painful. All I can do is hug her neck as tightly as my little arms can hold. They shake with the effort. It's painful.

It marks our barn. Then he smiled at me.

I look at papa. Desperate to catch his eye. Terrified of catching his eye. What will he call me? Janey? Jane? Young lady? Or will he say nothing and walk past me like I'm a shadow. Not a shadow! I'm terrified of being a shadow. Light kills shadows. Shadows evaporate into nothing.

Orange and red on black. The black advances and the orange fights back. Red cuts through. At what cost?

We know where to rebuild. We marked the spot. But…

Orange eats green grass, churns it into black dirt. Black takes the place of every other color. I grab mama so hard that she turns into a blanket. The spot that tells me where to return. Where to rebuild. It must be gone, too.

I hold tight to my blanket. It has a brown monkey on it. It doesn't belong to me. My blankets are gone. My mama is dead. This one belongs to Ann. She lives on the farm, and if I can find that spot, I can find them, too. The blanket tries to sail away, but I hold tight. I can't give it back to my grandchild if I lose it. I am floating across a black sky across a gigantic moon across the galaxies. White on black and the smash of something like glass holding something like water.

The blanket feels hot. Like a child with a fever. I had so many fevers. I hate fevers so much. They steal all your strength away and make nothing comfortable: not clothes, not beds, not a breeze, not a washcloth, not a glass of water, not a loving embrace. Shapes would dance on my walls. Ears of corn and stalks of wheat. Yellow corn and tan wheat. Scarecrows with smiling, pumpkin faces and overalls and straw hands. Red gloves. I only saw them in my fevers.

The blanket flies into a tree and catches in the branches. When I look up, it's not a tree but the stanza from a poem. I want to pull it out, so I can find the spot. But I might break the words. Words are so important after they're written down. The poem won't make sense, and the poet will be angry.

It's my poem. I can see that it's made out of fire and shadow, that's how I know. The blanket is wrapped around, and I tug the cloth like fire in my hands. Off goes the sentence. There is no longer a cold spot in his room. So where did his body used to be? I'll have to write a new sentence, a better one, to take its place. I'm not breaking the poem; I'm editing. I hold the sentence. It's long and hallow and easy to swing around. The letters are red and orange and black.

I start to fall. The blanket is not holding onto the poem. Falling takes forever, so I start running. I am going very quickly when two tree branches grab me around the middle and swing me up in the air to hang there like the moon. I look down, but I realize I might see papa's face, and I close my eyes just in time. He makes a siren noise. He shakes. He catches me and tosses me again. When I open my eyes, the moon is ready to consume me. I am flying right into the black circle of his mouth.

I hold tight to my words. I pinch the blanket with my knees. I jam the line into his mouth. I swing myself around and stand on my words. Cold is black, just like black is cold. Spot is orange, just like the spot was orange. I step on Spot, and it's also the other spot, so I can find my way home.

I'm standing on young men, lined up shoulder to shoulder and face down. They are dressed in black suits. Sliver of moon-white cloth stands out of their collars. At the end of line is a man dressed in black with diamonds in his hair. These men in black seem like my brothers, but they are not brothers. The man with diamonds seems like my father, but he is not my father. These men are my sons. The man is my husband. The men begin to turn, and I scramble to stay upright.

It wasn't supposed to burn down. Thank God we have the spot.

I lose my balance. The bodies of my sons and husband go spinning like tops and fly away. I land on the brown and green of ground, and it's daylight. I see the spot. I'm on Rebecca's farm, and I still have the blanket. The baby is in her room, laying on her tummy, waiting for her blanket.

I lay the monkey blanket across her. She is perfectly, impossibly still. The baby is Grace. Or Ruth. And maybe Ann, too. I retch and ache somewhere distant and forgotten. I can feel the cold from the crib, crawling up my arms. Trying to get down my throat. Trying to turn me into ice.

I run and run and run. I can't catch my breath. I turn back, and the house is gone. The farm is gone. And I'm in the skate rink. John skates up to me. "Ready for adventure?" he asks. His hair has stars in it. John closes his eyes, and his head begins to swell and swell, and it explodes.

I feel a hand on my arm, and I'm sitting next to Ethel in the cafe. She pats my arm. Her face says, "There, there, dear," but her lips say, "They aren't the only ones waiting for you." We look across the table. Jack is there. His neck is purple and black. The skin is twisted and ripped. His jaw is a wind-tapped hat, and his eyes swim with blood.

I stand up with a start and knock over the mug of coffee. It's cold. I choke on my words. I want to tell him hello, but my throat shuts up. Jack comes for me. He holds his arms out. I can't move. I'm wrapped in a blanket. He holds me, and the breath goes out of my lungs. Sharp pain in my side. He's crushing me. I feel my ribs crunch. I hear mushy snaps of old bones. His arms get warm the awful way secrets do.It's so hot next to his flesh. He's going to burn me alive.

Right here on the spot.

And I wake up.

A letter from John Becker, Sr. to Jane. Dated September 23, 1946.
—

Dear Jane,

My brother has never been happier. Maybe your cousin says the same thing. He's never been more in love, and I can't get him to stop raving about her in his letters. I'm starting to wonder if I should have married her. I heard they plan to drive to Canada for a honeymoon. They leave tomorrow. He's got lots to take care of at home, moving them in and all that. Guess he'll handle that when he gets back. For now, he says, they want to see the world.

You're probably wondering why I'm writing you. I know we only just met at the wedding, and it's only been three days, but I can't stop thinking about you. I've never been so knocked out by a woman before. You're so beautiful, and you're wicked smart. Chatting you up was like sword fighting.

I want to see you again, maybe start a courtship. I should have just stopped by, but I don't dare talk to you in person until I do some more reading. It's easier to do it this way, so you can't cut me to shreds if I stumble or blunder. This way, I can erase and start over until I feel safe enough to send it.

I'd like to take you out. Do you fancy a skate and some ice cream this weekend? Who doesn't? We can take my dad's car to the far side of the lake and skate until past dark. I'm not sure if you've ever been, but it's wonderful. You rent the skates there (no need to own your own pair).

If you're willing to take a chance on me, let me know by post or visit. I'll come by for you near five on Saturday. I'll buy us dinner at the skate rink, so come hungry and ready for adventure. Maybe, just maybe, we can make each other as happy as Jack and Ethel.

Yours truly,
John Becker

Jane sat at the kitchen table, writing. As soon as one was written and in an envelope, she was penning another. On the envelopes she wrote the names of her children. Lily and Junior pretended not to notice as they went about preparing for supper.

"Food's almost ready," Junior said. "I wonder when people will start showing up."

There was a knock at the door and a ring at the doorbell, nearly simultaneously. Then the doorbell rang again, six times in quick succession.

"I think the great-grandkids are here," said Junior. He wiped his hands on his apron and went to the front door. It swung open before he could touch the handle. Dane, six, and Madison, four, came bursting through with full arms at full speed.

"Hey, grandkids!" said Junior, breaking into a broad smile.

"Hey, grandpa," said the kids. They trudged past Junior and made their way into the kitchen. Behind them was Joseph, their dad, and Trisha, their mom.

"Hey, Joe," said Junior.

Joe smiled and gave his dad a hug.

"Hey, dad. Guess they're too busy to give you a proper hello."

"Yeah," Junior said, jerking a thumb behind him. "They went right for the kitchen."

Joe chuckled. "Any wagers on how long before Dane-"

"Grandma?" asked a small voice at Jane's side. "Did you make any bread pudding?"

Jane smiled down at the blond-haired, blue-eyed boy and nodded. His smile overcame his entire face. Jane smoothed the hair on his head, but he was gone, off to see what else there was to do. Madison, the spitting image of her brother, stepped forward into his vacancy. She smiled sweetly and threw her arms around Jane and said, "Hi, Grandma."

"Hello, Madison," Jane smiled back.

"Did you know we made a turkey in school?"

"You did?"

"Yup. Because of Thanksgiving."

"Wow. That's pretty special."

"Yup."

She danced a moment in place before deciding she had nothing else to say. She ran off as Joe and Trisha came in with their contributions. Joe marched into the kitchen to find empty counter space for his bags.

Trisha stopped at Jane's chair and bent to hug her.

"How are you doing?"

"Oh, okay."

Trisha gave the plaintive smile of a pained adult and held it for a moment before going to drop off her bags. Joe returned unsaddled and gave Jane a hug.

"Hey, grandma. Love you," he said giving her a peck on the cheek. "We brought veggies. They're boring, but someone's gotta keep this family healthy."

"Thank you, Joe."

Junior followed with a silver pot in his hands, then his wife, Hillary. Junior hurried past and found a burner to set the pot on. The routine repeated when Rebecca and Ivan showed up with their four: Brandon, Eli, Conrad and Ann on Rebecca's hip. The last to arrive was James who had walked from his apartment just down the street. They all made stops at the table, exchanged some condolence or simple affection.

It was a madhouse. The kitchen counter began to take on the appearance of a potluck. Junior had his ribs on a baking sheet next to a plate of burgers and hotdogs. It was all tented under hastily torn aluminum foil. There was a stack of yellow cheese nearby, and ketchup and mustard. Next to that were the buns and dinner rolls. Then came the mashed potatoes, creamy and white with flecks of red skin. The faint scent of garlic wafted up. Green bean casserole and creamed corn came next, then the veggie tray and fruit salad. Last in line was Jane's famous bread pudding. In the fridge were two pitchers of raspberry lemonade, one kept virgin for the kids, the other flavored with rum.

As the adults arranged and jockeyed their dishes, the kids ran and laughed and played in the living room. They were a literal blur of activity. Puzzles were out, and coloring books. Toys had been discovered from their various hiding holes. Many more things had been liberated from storage than children to play with them. Brandon and Eli were hovering over a twelve-thousand-piece puzzle they were spreading across a large folding table at the far end of the room. Conrad and Dane had cars and blocks out and were creating an elaborate obstacle course for the vehicles. Madison was on her stomach, marker in hand, coloring large swatches of a coloring book into a single color.

The door opened again, and Lily came in with two large white boxes in her arms. They were pie boxes with little cellophane windows. Lily used her foot to close the door behind her and plopped the boxes of pumpkin and apple next to the bread pudding. Joe reached over and slid the pies back, giving the bread pudding its proper placement.

"I mean, let's show some respect, Aunt Lily," he joked.

The energy settled at long last. Everyone else seemed to be standing. Jane was watching them all, and they were watching her.

"We should eat," she said. Junior nodded.

"Everyone come into the kitchen! We're going to pray!"

The children galloped in. They found spots clumped around doorway and near parents. Everyone folded their hands. When there was enough quiet, Junior crossed himself and said, "Bless us, oh Lord, and these thy gifts which we are about to receive. From thy bounty, through Christ our Lord." He paused for a long moment. "Special blessings on mom, the reason we're all here tonight, and every night. Amen."

Everyone did the sign of the cross. They started to migrate toward the food, but Junior went to Jane. He put a hand on her shoulder. Joe noticed. He put his hand on her other shoulder. Soon, everyone had hands on shoulders and arms and hands.

"Mom," Junior said, "we're all here because of you. You told me once that you sometimes felt boring, like you had no story to tell. But I see your story all around us. This family is your story. And it's a damn good one."

"Here, here!" shouted James.

Jane patted Junior on the hand.

"Um… why aren't we eating?" asked Madison, plate in hand.

"Good question, sweetie. Let's eat!"

A letter from Mary Jane Keller to her mother. Dated June 10, 1931.
—

Dearest mother,

My sweet darling Jane is sick again. Yes! Again! These boys of ours were born of mud and brick. They are hearty against these fickle winds and prevailing cold. My sweet darling Jane is a flower stem. Precious she is, and so fragile, too.

It began three days ago. She was in the garden with me, picking strawberries not yet ripe enough. When we came in, she looked rather flushed and red. Her forehead burned so! I soaked a cloth in water and held it to her face, but she seemed not to notice. That night it spread across her entire body. She was red all over like a strawberry. It was such a peculiar malady.

We dressed her for bed and waited for her color to come back. That night was not to be restful for any of us, I'm afraid. Jane thrashed and screamed all night. Her forehead was as hot as to burn my hands. She refused water and was ever sobbing and fighting unseen foes. We were all heartened to witness the sunrise, and with it her peace.

It has been three days now with Jane unable to rise from bed, so spent is she from the ordeal. She will sip water slowly but only after great convincing on our part. She has not eaten. The doctor believes it to be scarlet fever, and I've found myself wondering if the Lord is about to take my sweet darling Jane back to his bosom.

What am I to do? When will God heal my baby girl and bring her back to us? I pray the rosary daily as I sit at Jane's bed. Whenever I pass by, I cross myself and say a prayer. I wait for the Lord to deliver her from this illness with the Devil's impatience. What more can I do? I can only wait for the Lord to show me and guide me.

I had a dream that Jesus Christ came to me and comforted me about her. "Where is she?" I asked Him, for her bed was empty. "I've taken her with me. Her duties are fulfilled. She has confessed her sins and said her goodbyes. She is ready." I said, "How can that be, Lord? She's given me no such goodbye." But the Lord was gone, and I was alone again.

Mother, what would you do? Am I really so powerless to save her? Must I really put so much faith in the hands of others? I shall continue my little practice and pray to God and wait for my daughter to return to me. I shall wait and wait and wait, for the Lord works in his own time.

With all of my love,

Mary Jane

With the meal eaten, the children were excused and the family returned to the living room. Jane was in her chair again watching the television. In moments, the show came back to her, out of her memory. She had seen so many of these black-and-white westerns so many times that they felt like life experiences. That was part of what she liked about them. She could put herself back in her prairie dress and apron out on the farm, living her childhood again.

The cowboy confronted the native, who dashed off into the forest. The cowboy conferred with his fellow cowboys to discuss the matter. They were stuck there, with broken axels or injured oxen or something. That part she couldn't quite recall. Just that they couldn't leave and were forced into an uncomfortable native proximity. After the cowboy talked to the men, he went to his wife. She asked him pointed questions about the meeting. He gave terse, annoyed answers. She said their plan was suicidal and grabbed his arm. He shrugged her off. She offered a more diplomatic plan. She was told to stay put in the wagon, even if she hears gunshots. And then he left.

Jane thought of a pile of papers tucked away in a box in her bedroom.

It was quiet. Jane glanced around the living room, and it was empty. Jane's heart began to race. Was this how it happened? She had assumed death would come in the night, stealing her away while she slept. She never thought it could pounce upon her like this. She still had good-byes to say.

A hand snaked in from the hallway. It held the remote control. The TV clicked off, and the hand retreated. Jane could hear whispering. Then Madison came marching into the living room with a piece of paper in her hand. She meandered generally toward Jane, stopping to look at the whispers from the hallway for direction. Her face and body twisted with uncertainty. She held the paper out to Jane and said, "Here."

Jane reached forward and took the paper. It had two crudely drawn figures on it. They were touching hands. A beaming anthropomorphic sun hung in the sky above.

"What is it?" Jane asked.

"It's you and me. We're holding hands."

Jane beamed.

"Oh, it's very nice. Thank you."

A throat cleared from the hallway. Madison thought for a moment then jumped in place.

"Oh, right! I love your bathroom. It's so pretty."

"Oh, thank-"

Madison rushed forward into a weighty hug. The chair spun a little. Jane felt it in her side, but she tried not to notice. Madison she marched off, and Dane sprinted out next. His hands twisted and writhed behind his back. "I love your bread pudding. Yum!" He, too, rushed forward for a hug. Jane slipped a hand into her pocket and pulled out the recipe. She gave to him and sent him marching off.

Joe and Trisha came out together, their arms around each other. Joe said, "I love your straightforward honesty." Trisha said, "I love your flower garden. In the summer, more than right now." They gave their hugs and joined their kids.

Next came Conrad. "I love when you sing in church."

Eli said, "I love your puzzles and doing puzzles with you."

Brandon said, "Me, too." He came forward to give Jane a hug, but a voice from the hallway said, "No. Try again." Brandon slumped down a couple inches and backpedaled to the spot. "I mean, I love... your lasagna." Brandon gave his hug and ran off.

Rebecca, Ivan and Ann came out as a trio. Rebecca waved Ann's arm around. "I love your hugs," she said in a falsetto.

"And I love talking about farming with you," said Ivan.

"And I love how you teach me something new about cooking and raising a family every day."

They gave their hugs and stood to the side.

James waddled out next. He sighed and shook his head. "I love you, mom. I love that you love us, too, even if we make bad choices. I... I miss you already." His eyes were glassy as he went to the chair to give her a hug.

Hillary and John, Jr., came out next. Hillary touched a hand to her mouth. Her eyes were wet before she had said a word. She managed to say, "I love your fierce spirit." Junior rubbed his wife's back. "And I love... the hard work and ethics you bred into us, you and dad. It's made us all much better people than we could have been without it." They gave their hugs and joined the crowd.

Last out was Lillian. She was already crying. She stood before her mother with her hands at her sides. They were curled into fists. She took a deep breath. "I love that you gave us time: to live, to love and to say good-bye. I love you, mom."

The whole family moved in around her, wrapping her like a breath. At the center, the tiny, ailing woman, who was in the midst of her last day on earth, began to cry.

A letter from John Becker, Sr. to Jane. Undated.
—

Dear Blue J,

When you read this, I'll be dead. This is a hard letter to dictate, and I'm sure it's just as hard for Junior to write.

What can I say to you? You were a wonderful wife and are a fantastic mother. I will miss you more than anything in the world. I wish I could give you solace, but I can't. I can only die and end both of our suffering. But I don't do it willingly.

I know what it's like to die. I've never felt more betrayed. What began as confusion has unraveled everything for me. My body no longer obeys me. My thoughts no longer obey natural order. I fade in and out of the world. I always wonder how long I've been gone.

I would take about any other cancer than brain cancer. I know something is knocking over the furniture up there. What can I really trust? Not myself. Not my memories. Not my experience. Not even my words. We've been at this letter for an hour already.

I need to say thank you. You, alone, are the reason I'm still alive. You have been a wonderful, patient, selfless, beautiful caretaker for me. Because of who you are, I know our family will be just fine when I'm gone. I need to say that I'm sorry. I'm really truly sorry that this has happened to you and the kids. My death will leave its marks and scars on everyone. Only love and faith and hope can heal and carry on, but you must find that for yourselves.

I am ready. I've been fighting this cancer a long time now, and I'm done with it. I'm at a place where I'm ready to say that I've been beat. I'm very, very tired of trying to kill this thing that is so good at killing me. I am ready for us all to move on.

I hope that when the time comes for you, you'll be able to say good-bye. Never waste a good-bye. Make time for amends, final speeches and loose ends. You only get one chance to give peace to those you leave behind, so don't waste it. If you can't say it, write a letter. Find time for closure and move on with a lighter soul.

I love you. I love you. I love you. And I'll see you soon.

Dearest, deepest love,

John

Hands were stretched up and across and along the chair. The family was looking at Jane, watching her. She watched them back.

"How do you feel, mom?" Lily asked.

Jane shifted under the weight of hands.

"Fine. Tired."

Everyone stayed like that for a minute or two. But Jane didn't go anywhere. Gradually, hands returned. First, the youngest of them returned to their games and colors, older kids to puzzles and phones and comfortable seats. Jane's children began to scatter. Junior patted Jane's shoulder and found a spot near the fireplace behind Jane. Rebecca stood, swaying with Ann who had fallen asleep. James meandered into the kitchen. Lily stayed put, sitting on the floor next to the chair, her hand on her mom's hand.

They watched a western on television. She thought of her dad, building that gigantic barn. She thought of mother, relentless in her love and her concern. She thought of John, and her breath caught, so she looked away.

It was dark out. Jane looked to the east and the black windows reflected the inside of her house. Looking out was really looking in. She felt comfort. She felt the pressure of Lily's hand on hers, but she felt the presence of her entire family, visible and invisible.

Jane felt an exhilarating clarity to her senses suddenly. Her family members all had such unique energies, and she seemed to be experiencing them anew. She could feel it in the shades of her own energy, the way her life had given away life was imprinted on them. Even the smallest of them, even the ones she would never meet, were sealed by her mark, as she was by her parents and her grandparents and by all the other people rolled up in her family scroll. Jane knew her spirit stretched backwards through time to the first people, to the first living things, to first things ever. Energy is neither created nor destroyed, except once before and once forthcoming. Never was that more clear to Jane than in this strange personal seance in her living room.

This must be it, she thought.

Jane turned away from the TV and looked around. Lily was at her side. James was in the kitchen. Madison, Dane and Conrad were on the floor next to her chair. Rebecca stood with Ann over them. Ivan sat in the chair close to Rebecca. Hillary, Joseph and Trisha sat on the couch. John, Jr., sat on the eave of the fireplace. Brandon and Eli hunched over their puzzle at the far end of the room.

"Hey! Everyone! Come look at this!"

Jane turned to the kitchen. James was waving everyone over.

"I'm serious! You gotta see this!"

Everyone got up and herded into the kitchen. Jane saw the thin trails of color that connected her to these people. She saw that the strings connected her heart to theirs, and she knew that nothing can break that string. Lily patted Jane on the hand.

"Be right back, mom," she said.

Jane's hand felt cold. She snuck it back under her blanket. Her eyes wanted to close, but she wanted to watch the colors drip down the strings and disappear through the doorway. Tiredness came on. Jane was so much more tired than ever before. And cold. She drew the blankets around her, trying to keep as warm as possible. The lights were sneaking away, and the room was darkening.

"So many cardinals!"

"Is this normal?"

"Look! There's a bunch on our car!"

"It's so late. Why would they be flying around this late?"

Jane caught fragments of their excitement in the other room. Like the faraway songs of birds.

"Always on your terms, Blue J."

Jane tried to open her eyes, to see him. He sounded so near.

"John?"

"I've come to get you. Thought you could use a guide."

Jane fought her body. She brought the lights back a little.

"John? Where are you?"

"Close your eyes, Blue J. You'll see me a lot better."

"But…"

"I know. But it's time."

"What happens to them when I'm gone?"

"I think you saw for yourself that you won't be gone. Just like I wasn't gone. Those threads are pretty strong."

Jane couldn't open her eyes, but she could stop them from closing. The colors danced away from her.

"Aren't you happy to see me, Blue J?"

"Oh, John… I've never been happier."

"Oh, wow!"

"They're flying away!"

"Close your eyes, Blue J. It's time."

"Did anyone get a picture? We need to show mom."

"So beautiful…"
"I can't wait to show you around."
And Jane closed her eyes and rested in peace.

Made in the USA
Las Vegas, NV
14 January 2021